PRAISE FOR
MAVIS GALLANT'S FICTION:

"Compassionate in a tough-minded, unsentimental way, Gallant embraces humanity in all its foibles, flaws and foolishness."
– *Kitchener-Waterloo Record*

"Gallant has chronicled displaced lives with pulse-stopping mastery and has leavened her often painful message with reminders of the strength of human resilience. . . . Gallant is a master storyteller."
– *London Free Press*

"Mavis Gallant writes as the Dutch used to paint, filling each of her canvases, whether large or small, out to the edges with closely observed figures; some of them are amusing and others saddening, and all are bathed in an uncanny light that has nothing to do with the sun or moon but finds its source in an incandescent mind. . . . She leads us into a world where everything is ablaze and yet cool to the touch – a world of wit and pity mingled, where whatever the writer's eye falls on is made to yield a bittersweet, nourishing fruit."
– Brendan Gill

"Mavis Gallant is a master stylist with breathtaking powers of observation. . . . Gallant's stories are densely coloured worlds, spare and thorough. . . ."
– Montreal *Gazette*

"The satisfaction that comes from reading and re-reading Gallant's work lies in the lucid illuminations that arise from her compassionate portrayal of that inescapable junction where the political and the personal are indivisible."
– *Canadian Forum*

BOOKS BY MAVIS GALLANT

DRAMA
What Is to Be Done? (1983)

ESSAYS
Paris Notebooks: Essays and Reviews (1986)

FICTION
The Other Paris (stories, 1956)
Green Water, Green Sky (novel, 1959)
My Heart Is Broken (stories, 1964)
A Fairly Good Time (novel, 1970)
The Pegnitz Junction (stories, 1973)
The End of the World (stories, 1974)
From the Fifteenth District (stories, 1979)
Home Truths (stories, 1981)
Overhead in a Balloon (stories, 1985)
In Transit (stories, 1988)
Across the Bridge (stories, 1993)
The Moslem Wife (stories, 1994)
The Selected Stories of Mavis Gallant (stories, 1996)

MAVIS GALLANT

THE

PEGNITZ

JUNCTION

EMBLEM EDITIONS
Published by McClelland & Stewart Ltd.

Copyright © 1963, 1964, 1969, 1972, 1973 by Mavis Gallant

First published by Random House of Canada Limited, 1973
First Emblem Editions publication 2002

National Library of Canada Cataloguing in Publication Data

Gallant, Mavis, 1922-
The Pegnitz junction / Mavis Gallant.

ISBN 0-7710-3296-X

I. Title.

PS8513.A593P4 2002   C813'.54   C2002-901239-2
PR9199.3.G26P44 2002

We acknowledge the financial support of the Government of Canada
through the Book Publishing Industry Development Program for
our publishing activities. We further acknowledge the support of the
Canada Council for the Arts and the Ontario Arts Council for our
publishing program.

The following stories originally appeared in *The New Yorker*: "The Old
Friends," "O Lasting Peace," "An Autobiography," "Ernst in Civilian
Clothes," and "An Alien Flower."

SERIES EDITOR: ELLEN SELIGMAN

Cover design: Kong
Cover image: A. Hudson / Getty Images / Hulton Archive
Series logo design: Brian Bean

Typeset in Janson by M&S, Toronto
Printed and bound in Canada

EMBLEM EDITIONS
McClelland & Stewart Ltd.
The Canadian Publishers
481 University Avenue
Toronto, Ontario
M5G 2E9
www.mcclelland.com/emblem

1 2 3 4 5   06 05 04 03 02

CONTENTS

———◼———

THE
PEGNITZ
JUNCTION

The Pegnitz Junction

—■—

A Novella

She was a bony slow-moving girl from a small bombed baroque German city, where all that was worthwhile keeping had been rebuilt and which now looked as pink and golden as a pretty child and as new as morning. By the standards of a few years ago she would have been thought plain; she was so tall that she bumped her head getting in and out of airplanes, and in her childhood she had often been told that her feet were like canal boats. Her light hair would have been brown, about the colour of brown sugar, if she had not rinsed it in camomile and whenever possible dried it in sunlight; she could not use a commercial bleach because of some vague promise she had given her late grandmother when she was fourteen.

She had a striking density of expression in photographs, though she seemed unchanging and passive in life, and had caught sight of her own face looking totally empty-minded when, in fact, her thoughts and feelings were pushing her in some wild direction. She had heard a man say of her that you could leave her in a café for two hours and come back to find she was still smoking the same cigarette. She had done some modelling, not well paid, in middling ready-to-wear centers such as Berlin and Zurich, but now she was trying to be less conscious of her body. She was at one of those turnings in a young life where no one can lead, no one can help, but where someone for the sake of love might follow.

She lived with her family and was engaged to marry a student of theology, but the person closest to her was Herbert, who was thirty-one, divorced, and who with the help of a housekeeper was bringing up his only child. Unlike the student of theology, he had not put up barriers such as too much talk, self-analysis, or second thoughts. In fact, he tended to limit the number of subjects he would discuss. He had no hold on her mind, and no interest in gaining one. The mind that he constantly took stock of was his child's; apparently he could not be captivated in the same way by two people at once. He often said he thought he could not live without her, but a few minutes after making such a declaration he seemed unable to remember what he had just said, or to imagine how his voice must have sounded to her.

After they had known each other about seven months, they came to Paris for a holiday, all three of them – she, Herbert, and the child, who was called little Bert. Christine had just turned twenty-one and considered this voyage a major part of her emancipation. It was during the peak of a heat wave – the warmest July on record since 1873. They remained for a week, in an old hotel that had not been repainted for years because it was marked for demolition. They had two dusty, velvety rooms with a bathroom between. The bathroom was as large as the bedrooms together and had three doors, one of which gave on the passage. Leaving the passage door unlocked soon turned out to be a trick of little Bert's – an innocent trick; the locks were unlike those he was used to at home and he could not stop fiddling with them. The view from every window was of a church covered with scaffolding from top to bottom, the statue of a cardinal lying on its side, and a chestnut tree sawed in pieces. During the week of their stay nothing moved or was changed until a sign went up saying that a new car park was to be built under the church and that after its completion the chestnut tree would be replaced by something more suited to the gassy air of cities. The heat at night made sheets, blankets, curtains, blinds, or nightclothes unthinkable: she would lie awake for a long time, with a lock of her hair across her eyes to screen out the glare of a street lamp. Sometimes she woke up to find herself being inspected from head to foot by little Bert, who had crept to their room in search of his father. It was his habit to waken at two, and on finding the bed next to his empty, to come padding along in bare feet by way of the bathroom. Through her hair she would watch him taking a long look at her before he moved round the bed and began whimpering to Herbert that he was all alone and afraid of the dark.

Herbert would turn at once to little Bert. His deepest feelings were linked to the child. He sometimes could reveal anguish, of which only the child was the source. His first move was always to draw the sheet over Christine, to protect little Bert from the shock of female nakedness. Without a breath of reproach he would collect his dressing gown, glasses, watch, cigarettes, and lighter and take little Bert by the hand.

"I'm sorry," quavered the child.

"It's all right."

Then she would hear the two of them in the bathroom, where little Bert made the longest possible incident out of drinking a glass of water. The next day Herbert could not always recall how he had got from one bed to the other, and once, during the water-drinking rite, he had sleepily stuck a toothbrush in his mouth and tried to light it.

On their last night in Paris (which little Bert was to interrupt, as he had all the others) Herbert said he would never forget the view from the window or the shabby splendour of the room. "Both rooms," he corrected; he would not leave out little Bert. That day the Paris airports had gone on strike, which meant they had to leave by train quite early in the morning. Christine woke up alone at five. The others were awake too – she could hear little Bert's high-pitched chattering – but the bathroom was still empty. She waited a polite minute or so and then began to run her bath. Presently, above the sound of rushing water, she became aware that someone was pounding on the passage door and shouting. She called out, "What?" but before she could make a move, or even think of one, the night porter of the hotel had burst in. He was an old man without a tooth in his head, habitually dressed in trousers too large for him and a pajama top. He opened his mouth and screamed, "Stop the noise! Take all your belongings out of here! I am locking the bathroom – every door!"

At first, of course, she thought that the man was drunk; then the knowledge came to her – she did not know how, but never questioned it either – that he suffered from a form of epilepsy.

"It is too late," he kept repeating. "Too late for noise. Take everything that belongs to you and clear out."

He meant too *early* – Herbert, drawn by the banging and shouting, kept telling him so. Five o'clock was too *early* to be drawing a bath. The hotel was old and creaky anyway, and when you turned the taps it sounded as though fifty plumbers were pounding on the pipes. That was all Herbert had to say. He really seemed extraordinarily calm, picking up tooth-brushes and jars and tubes without standing his ground for a second. It was as if he were under arrest, or as though the porter's old pajama top masked his badge of office, his secret credentials. The look on Herbert's face was abstract and soft, as if he had already lived this, or always had thought that he might.

The scented tub no one would ever use steamed gently; the porter pulled the stopper, finally, to make sure. She said, "You are going to be in trouble over this."

"Never mind," said Herbert. He did not want any unpleasantness in France.

She held her white towelling robe closed at the throat and with the other hand swept back her long hair. Without asking her opinion, Herbert put everything back in her dressing case and snapped it shut. She said to the porter in a low voice, "You filthy little swine of a dog of a bully."

Herbert's child looked up at their dazed, wild faces. It was happening in French; he would never know what had been said that morning. He hugged a large bath sponge to his chest.

"The sponge isn't ours," said Herbert, as though it mattered.

"Yes. It's mine."

"I've never seen it before."

"Its name is Bruno," said little Bert.

Unshaven, wearing a rather short dressing gown and glasses that sat crookedly, Herbert seemed unprepared to deal with sponges. He had let all three of them be pushed along to Christine's room and suffered the door to be padlocked behind him. "We shall never come to this hotel again," he remarked. Was that all? No, more: "And I intend to write to the Guide Michelin and the Tourist Office."

But the porter had left them. His answer came back from the passage: "Dirty Boches, you spoiled my holiday in Bulgaria. Everywhere I looked I saw Germans. The year before in Majorca. The same thing. Germans, Germans."

Through tears she did not wish the child to observe, Christine stared at larches pressing against the frame of the window. They had the look they often have, of seeming to be wringing wet. She noticed every detail of their bedraggled branches and red cones. The sky behind them was too bright for comfort. She took a step nearer and the larches were not there. They belonged to her schooldays and to mountain holidays with a score of little girls – a long time ago now.

Herbert did not enlarge on the incident, perhaps for the sake of little Bert. He said only that the porter had behaved strangely and that he really would write to the Guide Michelin. Sometimes Herbert meant more than he said; if so, the porter might have something to fear. She began to pack, rolling her things up with none of the meticulous folding and pleating of a week ago, when she had been preparing to come here with her lover. She buckled the lightest of sandals on her feet and tied her hair low on her neck, using a scarf for a ribbon. She had already shed her robe and pulled on a sleeveless dress. Herbert kept little Bert's head turned the other way, though the child had certainly seen all he wanted to night after night.

Little Bert would have breakfast on the French train, said Herbert, to distract him. He had never done *that* before.

"I have never been on a train," was the reply.

"It will be an exciting experience," said Herbert; like most parents, he was firm about pleasure. He promised to show little Bert a two-star restaurant at the Gare de l'Est. That would be fun. The entire journey, counting a stopover in Strasbourg and a change of trains, would take no more than twelve hours or so; this was fast, as trains go, but it might seem like a long day to a child. He was counting on little Bert's cooperation, Herbert concluded sombrely.

After a pause, during which little Bert began to fidget and talk to his bath sponge, Herbert came back to the subject of food. At Strasbourg they would have time for a quick lunch, and little Bert had better eat his . . .

"Plum tart," said little Bert. He was a child who had to be coaxed to eat at every meal, yet who always managed to smell of food, most often of bread and butter.

. . . because the German train would not have a restaurant car, Herbert went on calmly. His actual words were, "Because there will be no facilities for eating on the second transport."

Christine thought that Herbert's information left out a great deal. Little Bert did not know what a two-star restaurant was, and would certainly have refused every dish set before him had he been taken to one. Also, the appalling schedule Herbert had just described meant that the boy would have nothing to eat or drink from about eleven in the morning until past his bedtime. She suggested they buy a picnic lunch and a bottle of mineral water before leaving. Her impression of the week just past was that little Bert had to be fed water all day and part of night. But Herbert said no, that the smell of food on trains made him – Herbert – feel sick. It was the thing he hated most in the world, next to singing. The train would be staffed with vendors of sandwiches and milk and whatever little Bert wanted. Herbert did not foresee any food or drink problem across the Rhine.

Well, that was settled, though leaving early had destroyed Herbert's plans for exposing the Louvre to little Bert and finding out what he had to say about the Postal Museum. "Too bad," said Herbert.

"Yes, too bad." She knew now that there had been only one purpose to this holiday: to see how she got along with little Bert.

Herbert let the child carry the sponge to the station, hoping he would forget it on the way. But he continued to address it as "Bruno" and held it up to their taxi window to see Paris going by.

"The porter seemed drugged," said Herbert. "There was something hysterical, irrational. What did he mean by 'too late'? He meant 'too early'!"

"He was playing," said little Bert, who had the high, impudent voice of the spoiled favourite. "He wanted you to play too."

Herbert smiled. "Grown people don't play that way," he said. "They mean what they say." His scruples made him add, "Sometimes." Then, so that little Bert would not be confused, he said, "*I* mean what I say." To prove it he began looking for the two-star restaurant as soon as they had reached the station. He looked right and left and up at a bronze plaque on the wall. The plaque commemorated a time of ancient misery, so ancient that two of the three travellers had not been born then, and Herbert, the eldest, had been about the age of little Bert. An instinct made him turn little Bert's head the other way, though the child could barely read in German, let alone French.

"I can't protect him forever," he said to Christine. "Think of what the porter said."

It was a sad, gnawing moment, but once they were aboard the express to Strasbourg they forgot about it. They had a first-class compartment to themselves. Herbert opened one smooth morning paper after the other. He offered them to Christine but she shook her head. She carried a paperback volume of Dietrich Bonhoeffer's essays tucked in behind her handbag. For some reason she thought that Herbert might tease her. They moved on to breakfast in the dining car, where Herbert insisted on speaking French. Little Bert was truly cooperative this time and did not interrupt or keep whimpering, "What are you saying?" He propped the object Herbert had begun to refer to as "that damned sponge" behind the menu card, asked for a drop of coffee to colour his milk, and ate toasted brioche without being coaxed. When the conductor came by to check their tickets little Bert suddenly repeated a French phrase of Herbert's, which was, "*Oh, en quel honneur?*" Everyone who heard it smiled, except Christine; she knew he had not meant to be funny, though Herbert believed the child had a precocious sense of humour. He did not go so far as to write down little Bert's remarks, but made a point of remembering them, though they were nothing but accidents.

The early start and the trouble at the hotel must have made Herbert jumpy. He kept lighting one cigarette after another so carelessly that sometimes he had two going at once. He looked at Christine and told her in French that she was overdressed. She smiled without replying; it was the end of the holiday, too late for anything except remarks. She glanced out at men fishing in ditches, at poplar shadows stretched from fence to fence, and finally – Herbert could tease her or not – she opened her book.

Little Bert was beside her in a second. He stood leaning, breathing unpleasantly on her bare arm. He laid a jammy hand over the page and said, "What are you doing?"

"Standing on my head."

"Don't," said Herbert. "Children can't understand sarcasm. Christine is reading, little Bert."

"But he can *see* that I'm reading, can't he?"

"What are you reading?" said the child.

"A book for an examination."

"When is it?" he said, as if knowing they had been expecting another "what?"

"In two days' time at eight in the morning."

Still he did not remove his paw from the page. "Can you read to me?" he said. "Read a story about Bruno."

"Herbert," she said suddenly, in her slow voice. "Do you ever think that nothing passes unobserved? That someone might be recording all your private expressions? The faces you think no one sees? And that this might be on film, stored away with tons and tons of other microfilm? For instance, your reaction to the porter – it wasn't a reaction at all. You were sleepwalking."

"Who would want a record of that?" said Herbert. "*En quel honneur.*"

"Read a story where Bruno has sisters and brothers," said little Bert.

"I'll read after Strasbourg," said Christine. She was too inexperienced to know this was a pledge, though Herbert's manner told her so at once.

"If Christine wants to study I'll read," he said.

Oh, he was so foolish with the child! Like a servant, like a humble tutor with a crown prince. She would never marry Herbert – never. Not unless he placed the child in the strictest of boarding schools, for little Bert's own sake. Was it fair to the child, was it honest, to bring him up without discipline, without religion, without respect, belief, or faith? Wasn't it simply Herbert's own self-indulgence, something connected with his past? It happened that little Bert's mother had run away. Not only did Herbert-the-amiable forgive his wife, but he sent her money whenever she needed it. In a sense he was paying her to stay away from little Bert. He'd had bad luck with his women. His own mother had been arrested and put in a camp when he was three. She had been more pious than political, one of a flock milling around a stubborn pastor. After she came home she would sit on a chair for hours, all day sometimes, munching scraps of sweet food. She grew enormous – Herbert recalled having to help her with her shoes. She died early and stayed in his mind as a bloated sick woman eating sugar and telling bitter stories – how the Slav prisoners were selfish, the Dutch greedy, the French self-seeking and dirty, spreaders of lice and fleas. She had gone into captivity believing in virtue and learned she could steal. Went in loving the poor, came out afraid of them; went in for the hounded, came out a racist; went in generous, came out grudging; went in with God, came out alone. And left Herbert twice, once under arrest, and once to die. Herbert did not believe for a second that the Dutch were this or the French were that; he went to France often, said that French was the sole language of culture, there was no poetry in English, something else was wrong with Russian and Italian. At the same time he thought nothing of repeating his mother's remarks.

Christine came up out of her thoughts, which were quite far from their last exchange. She said, "Everyone thinks other people are dirty and that they won't cooperate. We think it about the Slavs, the Slavs think it about the Jews, the Jews think it about the Arabs . . ."

Herbert said, "Oh, a Christian sermon? *En quel honneur?*" and stared hard at the two cigarettes lit by mistake and crowding the little ashtray. His mother's life had never been recorded, and even if it had been he would not have moved an inch to see the film. Her life and her death gave him such mixed feelings, made him so sad and uncomfortable, that he would say nothing except "Oh, a Christian sermon?" when something reminded him of it.

"Now, little Bert," said his father at eleven o'clock. "We are almost at Strasbourg. I know you are not used to eating your lunch quite so early, but we are victims of the airport strikes and I am counting on you to understand that." He drew the child close to him. "If there are shower-baths in the station . . ."

"We'll eat our plum tart," said little Bert.

"We'll have to be quick and alert from the time we arrive," said Herbert. He had more than that to say, but little Bert had put Bruno between his face and his father's and Herbert had no wish to address himself to a bath sponge. He began stuffing toothbrushes and everything they would need for their showers into his briefcase, not at all out of sorts.

Christine jumped down and made a dash in the right direction as soon as the train stopped. But the great haste recommended by Herbert had been for nothing: there were no showers. Nevertheless she paid her fee of one franc fifty centimes, which allowed her a threadbare dark-blue square of towelling, a sliver of wrapped soap, four sheets of glassy paper, and a receipt for the money. She showed the receipt to an attendant carrying a mop and a bucket and wearing rubber waders, who looked at it hard and waited for a tip before unlocking a tiled cubicle containing a washbasin. The tiles rose very high and the ceiling was lost in twilight. The place was not really dirty, but coarse and institutional. She took off her dress and sandals and stood on the square of towel. Noise from the platform seemed to seep between the cracked tiling and to swirl and echo along the ceiling. Even the trains sounded sad, as though they were used to ferry poor and weary passengers – refugees perhaps. The cubicle was as cold as a cellar; no sun, no natural light had ever touched the high walls. She stepped from the towel to her sandals – she did not dare set a foot on the cement floor, which looked damp and gritty. In these surroundings her small dressing case with its modest collection of lotions and soap seemed a wasteful luxury. She said to herself, If this is something you pay for, what are their jails like?

Outside she discovered a new little Bert, subdued and teary.

"He wanted his lunch first," said Herbert. "So we changed our plan. But he ate too fast and threw up on the buffet floor. Nothing has worked as we intended, but perhaps there will be some unexpected facility on the German train."

Little Bert held on to his sponge and hiccoughed softly. His face was streaked and none too clean. He looked like a runaway child who had been found in a coalbin and who was now being taken home against his will.

The German train crossed the Rhine at snail's pace and then refused to move another foot. Until it moved, the toilets and washrooms would be locked. They sat for a long time, discontented but not complaining, gazing out at freight sheds, and finally were joined by a man as tall as Herbert, wearing a blond beard. He had a thick nose, eyes as blue as a doll's, and a bald spot like a tonsure. He dropped his luggage and at once went back to the corridor, where he pulled down the top half of the window, folded his arms on it, and stared hard as if he had something to look at. But there was nothing on his side except more freight sheds and shell-pocked grey hangars. The feeling aboard this train was of glossed-over poverty. Even the plump customs man shuffling through seemed poor, though his regulation short-sleeved shirt was clean, and his cap, the green of frozen peas, rode at a proper angle. Something of a lout, he leaned out the window of their compartment and bawled in dialect to someone dressed as he was. Herbert sat up straight and squashed his cigarette. He was a pacifist and anti-state, but he expected a great deal in the way of behavior from civil servants, particularly those wearing a uniform.

Little Bert had been settled in one of the corner seats; the other was reserved for someone who had not yet appeared. Christine and Herbert sat facing each other. They were both so tall that for the rest of the afternoon someone or other would be tripping over their legs and feet. At last the freight sheds began to glide past the windows.

Christine said, "I don't feel as if I were going home." He did not consider this anything like the start of a conversation. She said, "The heat is unbelievable. My dress is soaked through. Herbert, I believe this train has a steam engine. How can they, when we have first-class tickets?" That at least made him smile; she had been outraged by the undemocratic Paris métro with its first- and second-class cars. Foul smoke streamed past the window at which the bearded man still stood. The prickly velvet stuff their seats were covered in scratched her legs and arms. The cloth was hideous in colour, and stamped with a pointless design. The most one could say was that it would do for first class.

"All we need here are lace curtains," Herbert remarked.

"Yes, and a fringed lampshade. My grandmother's parlour looked like this."

Little Bert, who seemed about to say what *he* thought of the furnishings, shut his mouth again; the owner of the window seat had arrived. This was an old woman carrying bags and parcels and a heavy-looking case that she lifted like a feather to the rack before Herbert could help. She examined her ticket to see if it matched the number at the window seat, sat down, pulled out the drop-leaf shelf under the sill, and placed upon it some food, a box of paper handkerchiefs, a bundle of post-cards, and a bottle of eau de cologne, all drawn from a large carryall on which was printed WINES OF GERMANY. She sprinkled eau de cologne on a handkerchief and rubbed it into her face. She had sparse orange-blond hair done up in a matted beehive, a long nose, small grey eyes, and wore a printed dress and thick black shoes. As soon as she had rubbed her face thoroughly she opened a plastic bag of caramels. She did not wait to finish eating one caramel before unwrapping the next, and before long she had her mouth full.

Christine said to Herbert in French, "The German train may have unexpected facilities." The air coming in at the window was hot and dry. The houses they passed looked deserted. "What would you call the colour of these seats?" she asked him.

"We've said it: middle class."

"That's an impression, not a colour. Would you say mustard?"

"Dried orange peel."

"Faded blood stains."

"Melted raspberry sherbet."

"Persimmons? No, they're pretty."

"I have never eaten one," said Herbert. He was not at all interested.

Little Bert spoke up and said, "Vomited plum tart," quite seriously, which made the woman in the corner say "Hee hee" in a squeaky tone of voice. "Read to me," said little Bert quickly, taking this to be universal attention.

"It isn't a book for children," Christine said. But then she saw that the woman in the corner was beginning to stare at them curiously, and so she pretended to read: "'It was the fourteenth of July in Paris. Bruno put on his blue-and-gold uniform with the tassels and buttons shining . . .'"

"No, no," said Herbert. "Nothing military."

"Well, you read then." She handed the book across. Herbert glanced at the title, then at the flyleaf to see if it was Christine's. He pretended to read: "'Bruno had a camera. He wore it on a strap around his neck. He had already dropped one in the lake so this one was not quite so expensive. He took pictures of Marianne, the housekeeper . . .'"

"'Who was really a beautiful princess instead of an ugly old gossip,'" said Christine.

"Don't," said Herbert. "She loves him." He went on: "'He took pictures of a little boy his own age . . .'"

"Is Bruno a bear or a boy?" said Christine.

"A male cub, I imagine," said Herbert.

"It's a sponge," said the offended child. He threw it down and went out to where the bearded man was still gazing at the dull landscape. All this was only half a gesture, for he did not know what to do next.

"That's sulking," said Christine. "Don't let him, Herbert. For his own sake make him behave." The woman in the corner looked again, trying to make sense of this odd party. Christine supposed that it was up to her to behave like a mother. Perhaps she ought to pick up the sponge, go out to little Bert, stoop down until their faces were nearly level and say something like, "You mustn't be touchy. I'm not used to touchy people. I don't know how to be with them." Or, more effectively, "Your father wants you to come back at once." She realized how she might blackmail little Bert if ever she married Herbert, and was ashamed. It was an inherited method, straight from her late grandmother's velvet parlour. But by now Herbert was trying to show little Bert something interesting out the window, and little Bert was crying hard. She heard the bearded man telling Herbert that he was a Norwegian, a bass baritone, and that he had been asked to teach a summer course in Germany. His teaching method was inspired by yoga. He seemed to expect something from Herbert, but Herbert merely mouthed "Ah," and left it at that. He was trying to get little Bert to blow his nose. Then, after an exchange she was unable to hear, all three

disappeared down the corridor, perhaps looking for a conductor. The toilets and washrooms were still locked.

A few minutes after this, at a place called Bietigheim, their
carriage was overrun by a horde of fierce little girls who had
been lined up in squads on a station platform for some time,
heels together and eyes front. Now there was no holding them.
"Girls, girls!" their camp monitor screamed, running alongside
the train. "Move along! Move along to second class!" They
took not the slightest notice; she was still calling and blowing a
whistle as the train pulled away.

Christine and the old woman sat helplessly watching while
their compartment was taken over by a commando, led by a
bossy little blonde of about eleven. Six children pushed into
the four empty seats, pulling up the armrests and making
themselves at home. "These places are taken," said Christine.
The commando pretended not to hear. All six wore knee-
length white lace socks and home-made cotton frocks in harsh
colours. For all their city toughness, they seemed like country
children. Their hair, loose and unbraided, was clasped here
and there with plastic barrettes. The child sitting in Herbert's
place had large red hands and the haunted face of a widow.
Another was plump and large, with clotted veins on her
cheeks, as if she were already thirty-five and had been eating
puddings and drinking beer since her wedding day. When she
got up suddenly the others giggled; the pattern of the first-
class velvet was imprinted on her fat thighs. As for the bossy
one, the little gangster, showy as a poppy in red and green, she
could not leave the others alone, but seemed compelled to
keep kicking and teasing them.

"No standing in first class!" This voice, growing louder and nearer, was so comically Bavarian that even the two adults had to laugh, though more discreetly than the children, who were simply doubled over. The voice was very like Herbert's, imitating a celebrated Bavarian politician addressing a congress of peasants. But Herbert was not unexpectedly being funny out there in the corridor, and the voice belonged to the conductor, now seen for the first time. He stumbled along saying "*No standing*," quite hopelessly, not really expecting anyone to obey, for who could possibly be afraid of such a jolly little person? He was only repeating something out of a tiresome rules book, and the children knew it. They leaned out the windows (also forbidden) trailing souvenir streamers of purple crêpe paper, past miles of larches with bedraggled branches, past a landscape baked and blind. The bossy blonde peeped out to the corridor and giggled and covered her mouth. She had small green eyes and resembled a thief. Yes, Christine could easily see her snatching something and concealing it – a ring left on a washstand, say. She took her hand away to offer a gap-toothed smile to Herbert, struggling along past girls and crêpe paper and long tangled hair and piles of luggage as if wading in seaweed. Instead of evicting the children at once he said a few comic words, which convulsed them anew, and asked for his briefcase. They would have murdered one another for the sake of being the favourite. The bossy blonde won, of course. She smiled adoringly. He appraised her as though she were twenty. All this took less than a minute. They were approaching Stuttgart.

The little girls filed off the train, leaving a curiously adult smell of sweat behind, followed by Herbert, the Norwegian, and little Bert. These three were still in pursuit of food and running water. She saw Herbert look at his watch. He had his briefcase in one hand and held on to little Bert with the other. The girls buzzed and swarmed. They seemed quite ordinary now; they were only children home from camp, waiting to be picked up by parents. The little gangster was overtaken by a mad mother pushing a pram and a grandmother who was the mother grown mean and fearful, plaintive and soft. The mother opened her thin mouth and cried to the little blonde, who was shaking hands all round with the friends she had so lately been abusing, "While you take hours to say goodbye to everyone, your poor grandmother is standing waiting . . ."

Waiting for what? said Christine to herself.

The grandmother put on the look of someone whose patience will never be rewarded enough. Her face said, No one need think *I* ask for favours. A lie, Christine decided. She asked for nothing but favours.

The once bossy, once confident little girl who had led the commando raid was all seriousness now, all worry, looking older than her grandmother ever would. She tried to say that she was sorry, but according to family timing it was too late. For a second longer Christine saw her small, upturned, elderly face.

"That was my grandmother," said Christine. "Such a black-mailer. So humble." She wondered if she had said this aloud, but the woman in the corner was busy with a chocolate bar and to all appearances had heard nothing except whatever went on in her own head.

Herbert and little Bert had not found everything they wanted at Stuttgart, but at least there had been time to brush their teeth. The Norwegian had become quite a friend of Herbert's now; at least, he seemed to imagine he had. He asked easily, casually, what Herbert's profession might be. Trying not to smoke, Herbert folded his hands and said he was an engineer. He described a method of clearing waste from rivers which consisted of causing an infinite number of tiny bubbles to rise from the bottom of the waters, each little bubble gathering and bearing upwards a particle of poisonous trash, which could then be raked off at the top. Herbert's information stopped there. If he had created an image of hand rakes, garden rakes, twig brooms; of women in bare feet and men in clogs raking away at the surface of ponds and inlets, he said nothing to change it. He was scrupulous about providing correct information but did not feel obliged to answer for pictures raised in the imagination. Christine thought that she knew what "information" truly was, and had known for some time. She could see it plainly, in fact; it consisted of fine silver crystals forming a pattern, dancing, separating, dissolving in a glittering trail along the window. The crystals flowed swiftly, faster than smoke, more beautiful and less durable than snowflakes. The woman in the corner said "Chck chck," admiring Herbert's method, and unfolded a new shopping bag labelled YOUR BEAUTICIAN HAS THE ANSWERS.

It was from the woman that the silvery crystals took their substance; she was the source. *It started this way*, Christine understood. She looked carefully at the woman who was creating information, all the while peeling paper stuck to a cream bun. She licked her fingers before taking the first bite. *This was the beginning. Two first cousins from Muggendorf married two first cousins from Doos. Emigrated to the USA, all four together. Two cousins, boy and girl, married to two cousins, girl and boy. The men got work right away in Flushing. Flushing was full of mosquitoes but these were got rid of in time for the World Fair. First factory ever to make good-class kitchen units for the unpretentious home. Disguised stove, vanishing sink, disappearing refrigerator, all that. First indoor barbecue, first electric spit for use in the smaller American residential facility. During the conflict the factory converted to making submarine gallery units, after the war reconverted to kitchen conveniences, all the wiser for the experience.*

The woman had finished her bun. She wet a handkerchief with eau de cologne, washed her hands and passed the handkerchief around the back of her neck. The trees rushing by were reflected in her eyes. *We never lived in Flushing because of the mosquitoes. Settled at once in Elmhurst and remained without a break for forty-seven years. Lived in a duplex residence. First rented then bought the upper, were later in a position to purchase the lower. Rented the downstairs place to white Lutherans of which there was no shortage. Never owned a car – never needed one. Never went anywhere. Other couple had bungalow with heated garage, car, large yard and barbecue. Never used the barbecue – she couldn't cook. Arrangement was that they would come to us for their evening meal. Had every evening meal together for forty-seven years. She didn't shop, couldn't market, never learned any English. I cooked around seventeen thousand suppers, all told. Never a disagreement. Never*

an angry word. Nothing but good food and family loyalty. I cooked
fresh chicken soup, pea soup with bacon, my own goulash soup, hot
beer soup, soup with dumplings, soup with rice, soup with noodles,
prepared my own cabbage in brine, made fresh celery salad, potato
salad our way, potato dumplings, duck with red cabbage, cod with
onions, plum dumplings, horseradish salad, sweet and sour pork our
way, goose giblets with turnips. Man in Brownsville made real
bratwurst, used to go over on Saturday to get it fresh. I made apple
cake, apple tart, apple dumplings, roast knuckle of pork, kidneys in
vinegar sauce, cherry compote our way, cheese noodles, onion tart,
trotters five different ways, cinnamon cookies, no brook trout – never
saw any real brook trout.

"Do you want to read to me?" said little Bert, seeing that
Christine was not doing anything in particular.

She opened the book with her customary slowness, which
seemed to irritate the child and drive him to refuse the very
thing he wanted. She said, "Bruno drives a racing car?"

"No."

"Bruno and the cowboys?"

"No."

"Bruno and the wicked stepmother?" This time Herbert
said "No" just as little Bert seemed about to say "Yes."

They came for dinner every night, at first on foot, then when they
got the car they would drive the three blocks.

She was saved from inventing more about Bruno by the
passage of one of the vendors Herbert had promised. Though
his trolley was marked "Coca-Cola," he had only a tepid local
drink to sell. He had no ice, no cups, and so few straws that
he was reluctant to give any away. Christine took a can of

whatever it was, and the one straw he grudgingly allowed her. She saw she had made a mistake: Herbert would not let little Bert have soft drinks, even in an emergency, because they were bad for the teeth, and of course he would not drink in front of the thirsty child. When she realized this she put the can down on the floor.

"Read!" said little Bert.

The woman in the corner, who had also bought a can of whatever it was, drank slowly, making a noise with her straw. *Nobody was ever as close as we were, two cousins married to two cousins. Never a cross answer, always found plenty of pleasant things to say.*

"I'm sorry about the drink, little Bert," said his father. "But you see, there are days when everything goes wrong from early morning, and even the weather is against you. That is what life is like. Of course it isn't like that *all* the time; otherwise people would get discouraged."

"Read out of your book," the child said, leaning on Christine. "Read how Bruno bit the other children."

"On the contrary, it says on this page that Bruno was an obedient sponge," said Christine. Raising her head, she looked at Herbert: "But sometimes on those days one feels more. More than just one's irritation, I mean. Everything opens, like a pomegranate. More things have gone wrong than one imagined. You begin to see that too."

"Little Bert has never seen a pomegranate," said Herbert. There were forms of conversation he simply refused to accept.

The woman in the corner had sucked up the last drops from the bottom of the can, and now began eating again. *Not only did I cook thousands of suppers, but they went on diets. Bananas and skimmed milk. The men lasted one day, she lasted two.*

"The Coca-Cola man," said little Bert – but no, this time the vendor had powdered coffee and a jug of hot water, which he was selling only to passengers who happened to have cups in their luggage; he had run out of plastic mugs. The woman pulled a pottery stein out of her WINES OF GERMANY bag and bought about an inch of coffee. Drinking it, she fanned herself with her chiffon scarf, complaining, "Too hot, too hot."

Half the time they all ate something different – this one rice, that one potatoes, the other one cornflakes and brown sugar. I was the one that stood there dishing it all up. Always on my feet. After she had finished the coffee she ate grapes, an apple, mint sweets, and raisin cookies. *I never got used to the electric stove. But I had to have it electric. It came from the factory.*

A smell of rot began to fill the compartment. The grape seeds and stems, the apple core, and the papers the sweets had been in had immediately become garbage. The Norwegian was clearly disturbed – nauseated, in fact. He kept moving in and out to the passage, trying to catch the slightest breath of fresh air. Each time he came back he stared at Christine.

Christine was conscious of her bare brown arms because she could see the Norwegian eyeing them. She raised them, nervously toying with her scarf. Herbert sat as calm as an incarnation of Buddha, even when their direction changed and the sun fell directly on him; even when the woman beside him shut the window because the hot breeze touched her beehive of hair. He must have been as hot and uncomfortable as the rest of them, but nothing would ever make him say so.

To escape the Norwegian's staring, Christine went out to the corridor and stood with her arms resting on the lowered window. She could see a road, a low wall, and a private park filled with shade trees sloping up to a small mock-Gothic castle built of reddish stone. Two cream-coloured cars were drawn up before the gates – the Mercedes belonging to Uncle Ludwig and a Volvo driven by the horrible Jürgen, who was Uncle Ludwig's contact man. Jürgen was large and strong, weighed more than two hundred pounds, and had a beaked nose and eyes so sunken he looked blind.

It was like Uncle Ludwig to make everyone get out at the gates instead of driving straight in. He still dressed as he had when he was poor; he had on the trousers of one suit and the jacket of another, a narrow tie bought years ago out of a barrow, and metal-tipped boots. His clothes tended to be loose-fitting because he carried wads of money all over his person, paid everything in cash, kept his records in his head. Uncle Ludwig never carried a gun; Jürgen did. Along with these two, the party included Uncle Bebo, Aunt Barbara, Aunt Eva, Uncle Max, and Uncle Georg with Aunt Milena. These two were father and mother to a little boy who got out last of all and gave his hand to a grandmother. Grandmother was dressed in a long skirt and a blouse of dark blue embroidered with daisies of a lighter blue, so small they looked like dots. Upon the skirt was an apron of yet another blue, with a hem of starched glossy pleats. She was in shades of blue from her chin to her wrists and right down to the tops of her shoes, which were black and polished, without buckles or any nonsense. Grandmother had a wide mouth, eyes like currants, high cheekbones, and a little blunt nose. She was not much taller than her grandson.

The whole party shook itself out. The women straightened their skirts and blew what they hoped would be cooler air on each other's necks; the men wiped their wet foreheads with folded handkerchiefs and replaced their hats. They turned at the same time and smiled their respects to the estate steward, who had a broken neck and wore a cast like a white chimney. Close behind him came a thin man in country tweeds; he looked to them more English than German, because of all the aristocratic British scoundrels they had seen in films. He strolled down to them with his feet hidden in a low cloud of housedogs, who did not let up barking. He was not English, of course, but as removed from them as any foreigner might have been. He spoke with such a correct and beautiful accent that Grandmother could make out only a word or two. She looked away, blushed, and performed a deep curtsey.

Jürgen muttered, "The family came for the drive," to which the steward said affably that they could visit, with a great wave that seemed to waft them up the green hill and indoors.

"The castle is a museum," said Uncle Bebo. He was the only one in the family who had travelled much in peacetime.

Uncle Ludwig, who always sounded like a piece of metal machinery, said, "Yes – visit!" which was something of an order. He and his man Jürgen had come here to see about buying thousands of Christmas trees for the market next December. The steward, part of whose job it was to talk about money, removed himself to an alley of lime trees with the horrible Jürgen, while Uncle Ludwig and the thin man sat down on a stone bench carved with pineapples and began a discussion about the cathedral at Freiburg. Uncle Ludwig did not know if he had ever seen the cathedral or only pictures of it, and did not care whether he had or had not. Now that he was rich he was not thought ignorant any more, but simply eccentric. He sat patiently, letting Jürgen get on with it.

The rest of the party marched on to the castle, led by Uncle Bebo. Knowing about museums, Uncle Bebo had some loose change ready, five marks in all, with which to tip the guide. It was a long walk, all uphill. The hot weather, plus Uncle Bebo's jokes, made them feel silly and drunk. Giggling and hitting each other, they trooped in and up a great flight of stairs – Uncle Bebo said that in castle-museums the ticket office was one floor up. They opened doors on museum rooms furnished to look as if someone lived in them. Uncle Bebo fingered the draperies and even tried the beds, while Aunt Barbara, who had one problem on outings, and one only, began to look for a sign saying "Ladies."

"That will be downstairs," much-travelled Uncle Bebo said. He led the descent, opened another great door, and saw what he took to be the staff of the museum eating lunch. He swung his arm back, the confident gesture of a know-it-all, and the others followed him into a large dining room where some ten or twelve persons of all ages stared back at them without speaking.

"Good appetite!" the visitors cried. They urged the staff to take no notice, please – to eat up their veal and dumplings while the dish was still hot. Uncle Bebo tried to see if the guide to be tipped was here, but none of the stunned faces showed the required signs of leadership. The men at lunch wore country jackets with bone buttons. The women seemed so dowdy that nobody remembered later what they were wearing. The visitors were in their Sunday urban best – meaning, for the aunts, pinkish nylon stockings, flowered drip-dry frocks, white no-iron cardigans, Aunt Barbara in a no-iron skirt from Italy and shoes with needle heels and her hair rolled up in blond thimbles. The men wore high collars and stiff shiny ties, had hair newly trimmed so that a crescent of skin left each ear looking stranded. The men smelled of aftershave lotion – lilac and carnation – that they'd been given last Christmas by the family women.

The visitors followed Uncle Bebo once around the table. They paused when he did, to squint at an oval portrait, nodded when he said, "Baroque!" and cried out with wonder at the sweet bell-tone when he snapped his fingernails on a crystal punchbowl – all the while renewing their smiles and encouraging remarks to the staff. Finally all headed towards another door at the end of the room. This one had a pointed lintel beneath which Uncle Bebo paused for the last time. He raised his fist (still clenched around the five marks), looked up at the lintel, back at the frozen people of all ages clutching their knives and forks, did not cry, "Death to upper-class swine!" as they might have feared in their collective bad dream, but only, "This door is Gothic! No mistake!" and led the visitors on, the marks in his knuckles going *cling-cling-cling*. Granny turned back, smiled, curtsied deeply, and gave them a blessing.

Now they began to look for THIS WAY OUT, for there had not been all that much to see in the museum. Aunt Barbara was still watching for the door she wanted. Uncle Bebo clamped his teeth together and made a hissing sound to torment Aunt Barbara, so that she couldn't stop laughing, which was no help either. All at once they were outside again in the handsome park, with Aunt Barbara searching hard for a row of shrubs or a tree large enough to conceal her. As soon as she saw what she needed she cried to her mother-in-law, "Oh, Granny, a lovely tree, a thick fat beautiful tree," and galloped off, hiking up her Italian pleated skirt. The grandmother was slower, bothered by her long petticoats – two of them navy blue, two of white linen-and-cotton, one of lawn – and mysterious bloomers that were long in the leg and had never been seen by her own daughters: they were washed apart, hung to dry between pillow cases, and ironed by Granny in the dead of night.

Granny grasped the edge of the innermost petticoat. The trick was to bundle all the other skirts within it and hang on to the hem with her teeth. Just as she had a good hold on the hem she happened to see two boys of sixteen or so running with large black dogs on leads in and out of shade down the sloping lawn. The dogs were barking and the boys were calling to the women, "Stop! Stop!"

But then from far away, from within the alley of lime trees, another cry sounded, and, running too, breaking free of the trees, came the steward, the horrible Jürgen, then sly-eyed Uncle Ludwig, and the owner of the trees with his little cloud of house dogs. Before these two parties could meet and lambaste each other with sticks and fists it was established that the ugliest of the intruders – Uncle Ludwig – was that Godsent figure who might purchase thousands of Christmas trees. The boys backed off, pulled their dogs in short, and said, "We didn't know."

Aunt Barbara seemed thoroughly pleased to see everyone; she always liked a crowd. But she was bothered because her skirt was not hanging as she wanted it to, her undergarments having become tangled and twisted. She had to unzip the placket of her skirt, so that it looked as if she meant to take it off; but all she did was give a good wiggle and shake, and when everything had settled she zipped it up again and cried, "Oh, the dear sweet beautiful dogs!" So everything ended well, and as the two boys led Granny back up to the little castle, through the still sunny day filled with such exquisite green lights and shadows, she could be heard saying that she had known all along it could not have been a museum; the beds looked too soft.

Now all this family of visitors save one, the child, were struck dead before long. Five of them carried the germ of the cancer that would destroy them, and one died of a stroke. The little boy was allowed to grow up, but his parents were killed when a military helicopter exploded over a crowded highway on a Saturday afternoon. As for the horrible Jürgen, he was found murdered in a parking lot. A man who signed an IOU for five hundred marks in Jürgen's favour disappeared one day. The man's wife said he was dead, but Jürgen had yet to see an account of the funeral. He grew tired of waiting and went to call on the widow. She was obstinate, said she knew nothing about a debt, that her husband was buried. The death certificate had been lost. There was no stone on the grave because she had no money to pay for one. When she began to contradict herself, turned vague and weepy, Jürgen gave up talking and looked to see what he could take instead of the money. He lifted a coffee table out of the way and began rolling up a small rug. All the while he was doing this the widow howled that it was her best carpet, the only thing she owned worth selling. True – everything else was trash, probably bought second-hand to begin with.

Instead of crossing the road to the parking lot Jürgen strode down to the corner and the traffic lights (he was law-abiding) and around the corner; made a detour to compare his new rug with some in a store window; turned up a side street and back to the parking lot across from the widow's place. There he saw one of her sons, aged about thirteen. "What now?" Jürgen sang out. He held the rug overhead, thinking the kid would grab for it. He was good-tempered, laughing. He had an advantage; not only was he powerful and large, but he was not afraid of harming anyone.

The kid broke into a run, with a hand behind his back.

"You don't want to do that," said Jürgen. He was ready to cripple the kid with a knee and step on his right hand, but only if he had to. He must have seemed like a great statue to the boy, standing with both arms straight up supporting the carpet. Jürgen brought his knee up too high and too soon; he was used to fighting with men. The kid bent gracefully over the knee and pushed the length of the blade of a kitchen knife above the buckle of Jürgen's belt.

The train trembled and slid round a curve, out of sight of the dappled lawn and the people climbing slowly up to the castle, on their last excursion together. Christine moved back to the compartment to make way for a vendor in a white coat pulling an empty trolley.

"We have had drinks without ice," said Herbert. "Coffee without cups. Now nothing at all."

The woman in the corner fanned herself briskly with a fan improvised out of postcards. *They came over every night and for lunch on Sundays. When the other couple had God's own darling, our precious Carol Ann, they would bring her in a basket lined with dotted Swiss. I remember Carol Ann's first veal cutlet. I had a wooden hammer – no American butcher knew how to slice veal thin enough. Later they went on their diets, wanted broiled steaks, string beans, Boston lettuce, fat-free yogurts. Carol Ann the little cow came home from summer camp with a taste for cold meat loaf made from stray cats and chili sauce. The little bitch grew older, demanded baker's cakes, baker's pies, cupcakes in cellophane, ready-mix peach ice cream, frozen lasagna, pineapple chunks, canned chop suey, canned spaghetti, while the big cow, the little cow's mother, got a craving for canned fudge sauce their way, poured it over everything, poured it over my fresh spicecake. I stopped making spicecake.*

"We could move, you know," said Christine to Herbert. "I've noticed one or two empty compartments."

"I have seen them too," said Herbert, "but the seats in those compartments have been reserved and we would eventually have to come back here."

"It's just that I don't feel well," she said.

"Heat and hunger and thirst," said Herbert. He shrugged, though not through indifference; he meant that he was powerless to help.

They wanted Aunt Jemima pancakes, corn syrup, maple syrup, hot onion rolls, thousand-island dressing, butter that would give you jaundice just to look at, carrots grated in lemon Jell-O, and as for the piglet Carol Ann, one whole winter she would not eat anything but bottled sandwich spread on ready-sliced bread, said only Jews and krauts and squareheads ate the dark. Had been told this by her best friend at that time, Rose of Sharon Jasakowicz.

"There's too much interference!" said Christine, though little Bert was not being a bother at all, was nowhere near her. She sprang up and went back to the corridor, untied her scarf and let the wind lift her hair. The Norwegian stood close beside her and showed her his yoga method of breathing, pinching his nostrils and puffing like a bullfrog. The train stopped more and more erratically, sometimes every eight or nine minutes. Presently she noticed they were standing in a stationyard that seemed so hopeless, so unlikely to offer even the most primitive sort of buffet, that none of them made a move to go out. The yard buildings were saturated with heat, grey with drought, and the shrubs and trees beyond the station contained not a drop of moisture in their trunks and stems. A loudspeaker carried a man's voice along the empty platform: "All the windows on the train are to be shut until further orders."

"They can't mean this train," said the Norwegian.

Herbert, evidently annoyed by such a senseless direction, immediately went off to find the conductor. The woman in the corner began peeling an orange with her teeth. "I have diabetes, I am always hungry," she said suddenly, apparently to little Bert.

Herbert soon came back with an answer: there had been grass and brush fires along the tracks. "They may even have been set deliberately," he said. She could hear him explaining calmly to little Bert about the fires, so the child would not be alarmed.

"We can't shut all the windows in this heat," said Christine. "Certainly not for long." No one answered her.

After the train had quit the grey stationyard she continued to stand at the open window, her hair flying like the little girls' purple crêpe-paper streamers. Each time the train approached a curve she imagined the holocaust they might become. She thought of the ties consumed, flakes of fire on the compartment ceilings, sparks burned black on the first-class velvet. All the same, she kept hold of the two window handles, ready to slide the pane up at the first hint of danger. No one challenged her except for the bun-faced conductor, who asked if she had heard the order.

"Yes, but there aren't any fires," she said. "We need air." It was true that there were no signs of trouble except for burned-out patches of grass. Not even a trace of ash remained on the sky, not even a cinder. The conductor continued to look at her in his jolly way, head to one side, a smile painted on his face, looking as round and as stuffed as a little clown. "All right," she said. "I shall close the window, at least until Backnang. Then you can say that we all obeyed you."

"The train has been rerouted because of the danger," he said. "No Backnang."

"That seems fairly high-handed of you," she began, but of course she was wasting her breath. He was only a subaltern; he had no real power.

With its shut window, the compartment was unbearable now. Even little Bert was looking green.

"I was going to tell you about the change," said Herbert. "But you were having a yoga lesson and I didn't want to interrupt. We go through Coburg now. We shall be a couple of hours late, I imagine. I believe we change trains. Coburg is a pretty place," he added, to console her.

"Will it be explained at the station at home?" she said. "Someone is supposed to be meeting me."

"Meeting *us*," Herbert corrected, because in the eyes of these strangers he and Christine were married. The truth was that they would separate at their home station as if they were strangers.

The woman in the corner emptied one of her plastic bags of all the food it contained and filled it with the rubbish. *Sundays I had them for the two meals. They wanted just soup for supper, with cold ham and iceberg lettuce, dressing their way. The men ate Harvard beets in the factory canteen; they started wanting them. They wanted two or three different kinds of pizzas, mushroom ketchup, mustard pickles.*

Little Bert kept an eye on Christine. "You never finished reading," he said.

"I can't remember what I was reading about," she said.

"What is the book called?" he said.

"*All About Bruno*," said Christine. "What else could it be?"

"No, that might confuse him," said Herbert. "He knows Bruno is his own invention. The book is supposed to tell Christine how to think, little Bert. The Bruno story might be there. I don't say it is."

"Now who is confusing?" said Christine.

"But *is* the Bruno story inside?" said little Bert. "Look again," he urged Christine.

She looked, or pretended to. "Bruno goes to the moon?"

"No, I know about the moon."

"Bruno goes to an anti-authoritarian kindergarten?"

"Don't tease him," said Herbert.

"The kindergarten," said little Bert. He leaned against her, out of fatigue, apparently. She might have felt pity for the fragile neck and the tired shadows around his eyes, but there were also the dirty knuckles, the bread-and-butter breath, the high insistent voice.

During the depression the factory laid off, nobody was buying the kitchen units. I went to collect the relief, he was too ashamed. They didn't send you cheques in those days, you had to go round and see them. The other couple still came for dinner. We ate beans, sardines, peanut butter, macaroni. You could get lambs' kidneys for twenty cents, nobody in the USA ate them. Also heart, tongue. He was laid off from February 16, 1931, to September 23, 1932. Went back part-time. I did part-time work cooking in Carol Ann's school. She called me "Mrs.," would never say I was a relative. My cousin-in-law never worked, always had headaches, had to lie down a lot, never learned English. Then the factory picked up full speed, getting ready for the conflict. I fed them all through the war, stood at the electric stove, making oxtail soup on the one hand, baked squash on the other, bread and milk when my cousin had his ulcer.

"I have something he might like to look at," the woman in the corner said. She offered little Bert part of her collection of postcards, but he put both hands behind his back and pressed even closer to Christine. Taking no notice of him, the woman began handing the cards around clockwise, starting with Herbert. "My friends on their summer holidays," she said. Herbert passed on the dog-eared coffee-stained views of Dubrovnik, Edinburgh, Abidjan, Pisa, Madrid, Sofia, Nice. "Very nice," she said, encouraging Herbert. "Very nice people."

The Norwegian looked at each card seriously, turned it over, examined the stamp, read the woman's name and address, and tilted the card at an angle to read the message. The messages were aslant, consisted of a few words only, and ended in exclamation marks. He read aloud, "'Very nice friendly people here!'"

The woman was smiling, handing the cards around, but her mind was elsewhere. *We never took the citizenship so we never voted. Were never interested in voting. During more than forty years we would only have voted four times anyway. Would have voted:*

In 1932 – for Repeal.

In 1936 – against government interference and wild spending. Against a Second Term.

In 1940 – against wild utterances and attempts to drag the USA into the conflict on the wrong side. The President of the USA at that time was a Dutch Jew, his father a diamond cutter from Rotterdam, stole the Russian Imperial jewels after the Bolshevik revolution, had to emigrate to avoid capture and prison sentence. Within ten years they were running the whole country. Had every important public figure tied up – Walter Winchell, everybody. Their real name was Roszenfeldt.

In 1944 – against a Fourth Term. My cousin had a picture, it looked like a postcard, that showed the President behind bars. Caption said, "Fourth Term Hell!!!!!! I'm in for Life!!!!!"

Apart from those four times we would never have voted.

"We are on an electric line again," Herbert told little Bert, who could not have had the faintest idea what this meant. The child looked wilted with heat. Their conductor had opened all the windows – there seemed to be no further news about fires – but nothing could move the leaden air.

"I want it all in order," Herbert said to Christine. "I really do intend to write a letter. Most of the toilets are still locked – true? There isn't a drop of drinking water. The first vendor had no ice and no paper cups. The second had nothing but powdered coffee. The third had nothing at all. All three were indifferent."

"True," said the woman, answering in place of Christine. She took off her black shoes and put her feet on top of them as if they were pillows.

The conductor returned to check their seat reservations for the third or fourth time. "This is only a flag stop," he said, as their train slowed. To make it easier for him, those who were in the wrong places – Christine, the Norwegian, and little Bert – moved to where they were supposed to be. The train was now inching along past a level crossing, then gave a great groan and stopped, blocking the crossroad. The barriers must have been down for some time because a long line of traffic had formed, and some of the drivers, perspiring and scarlet, had got out to yell protests and shake their fists. The sight of grown people making fools of themselves was new to little

Bert, or perhaps the comic side of it struck him for the first time; he laughed until he was breathless and had to be thumped on the back. The woman in the corner kept an apple between her teeth while she looked in her purse for the ticket. Her eyes were stretched, her mouth strained, but there was no room on the table now, not even for an apple. As for the three men – Herbert, the conductor, and the Norwegian – something about the scene on the road had set them off dreaming; the look on their faces was identical. Christine could not quite put a name to it.

The woman found her ticket and got rid of the apple.

My husband said that if the President got in for a Fourth Term he would jump in deep water. That was an expression they used for suicide where he came from, because they had a world-famous trout stream. Not deep, though. Where he came from everybody was too poor to buy rope, so they said the thing about jumping. That was all the saying amounted to.

To be truthful, said Christine to herself, all three of them seem to be thinking of rape. She wondered if the victim could be the pregnant young woman – a girl really, not as old as Christine – who was running along beside the tracks, making straight for the first-class carriage. Probably not; she was unmistakably an American army wife, and you could have counted on one hand the American wives raped by German men. There existed, in fact, a mutual antipathy, which was not the case when the sexes were reversed. *But* – here Christine imitated Herbert explaining something – we are not going to explore the attraction between German girls, famous for their docility, and American men, perhaps unjustly celebrated for theirs. We are going to learn something more about Herbert.

Christine suddenly wondered if her lips had moved – if it was plain to anyone that her mind was speaking. At that second she noticed a fair, rosy, curly, simpering, stupid-looking child, whose bald and puffy papa kept punching the crossing barrier. Julchen Knopp was her name. Her skirt, as short as a tutu, revealed rows of ruffled lace running across her fat bottom.

They brought up the heiress Carol Ann American style – the parents were chauffeur and maid. The mother couldn't be chauffeur because she never learned to drive. My husband was crazy about Carol Ann. He called her Shirley Temple. I called her Shirley Bimbo, but not to her face.

At some distance from the smirking Julchen, agape with admiration but not daring to speak, stood four future conscripts of the new anti-authoritarian army: they were Dietchen Klingebiel, who later became a failed priest; Ferdinandchen Mickefett, who was to open the first chic drugstore at Wuppertal; Peter Sutitt, arrested for doping racehorses in Ireland; and Fritz Förster, who was sent to Africa to count giraffes for the United Nations and became a mercenary.

What she had just seen now was the decline of the next generation. What could prevent it? A new broom? A strong hand? The example of China? There was no limit to mediocrity, even today: the conductor had lied too easily; this was nothing like a flag stop. They had been standing still for at least seven minutes. Punctilious Herbert was far too besotted with Julchen Knopp to notice or protest. She felt an urgent need to make him pay for this, and tried to recall what it was he had said he hated most, along with the smell of food in railway compartments. As soon as they were moving again and the conductor had left off staring and gone away, she turned to the Norwegian and said, "Do please show us your yoga breathing method, and do let us hear you sing."

"Some people imagine that yoga is a joke," said the Norwegian. "Some others don't care about singing." Nevertheless he seemed willing to perform for Herbert and little Bert and the insatiable passenger in the corner. He shut the door, which instantly made the compartment a furnace, sat down where little Bert should have been, pinched his nostrils between thumb and forefinger and produced the puffing bullfrog sounds Christine had already heard. He let his nose go and said in a normal voice, "I sing in five languages. First, a Finnish folk song, the title of which means 'Do Not Leave,' or 'Stay,' or 'Do Not Depart.'" He looked at Herbert. Perhaps he knew that Herbert had been teasing Christine, calling the Norwegian "your bearded cavalier."

The Norwegian pulled out the drop leaf at his end of the window and beat a rhythm upon it. His eyes all but vanished as he sang. His mouth was like a fish. As for Herbert, he suddenly resembled little Bert – eyes circled and tired, skin over the temples like tissue paper. She thought that he must be exhausted by the heat and by his worry over the child, and she remembered that although he hated the smell of food he had not said a word about it. The singing was tiring, finally; it filled the compartment and seemed to leave everyone short of breath. She got up and crossed to Herbert's side, and he, with the Norwegian's eyes fixed upon him, began stroking her arm with his fingertips, kissing her ear – things he never did in public and certainly not in front of little Bert. She sat quite still until the voice fell silent.

The woman in the corner and little Bert applauded for a long time. Herbert said, "Well. Thank you very much. That was generous of you. Yes, I think that was generous . . ."

Having said what he thought, Herbert got up and left abruptly, but nobody minded. All of them, except for the woman, departed regularly in search of a drink, a conductor, or an unlocked washroom. Little Bert curled up with his face to the wall and began to breathe slowly and deeply. The Norwegian, still in little Bert's seat, tucked his head in the corner. His hands relaxed; his mouth came open. His breathing was louder and slower than the child's. From the corner facing his came *First the block around us got Catholic then it got black. That's the way it usually goes. I can tell you when it got Catholic – around the time of Lend-Lease. We remained in the neighbourhood because there was a Lutheran school for the child. Good school. Some Germans, some Swiss, Swedes, Norwegians, Alsatians, the odd Protestant Pole from Silesia – Rose of Sharon was one. Seven other girls were called Carol Ann – most popular name. Later Carol Ann threw the school up to us, said it was ghetto, said she had to go to speech classes at the age of twenty to learn to pronounce "th." Much good did "th" do our little society queen – first husband a bigamist, second a rent collector. Th. Th. Th.*

This was followed by a dead silence. Herbert beckoned Christine from the corridor. She thought he wanted to stand at the window and talk and smoke, but he smiled and edged her along to one of the empty compartments at the end of their carriage. They sat down close together out of the sun and in a pleasant draught, for there was no one here who could ask them to shut the window. But then Herbert slid the door to, and undid the plushy useless curtains held back by broad ties. The curtains were too narrow to meet and would serve only to attract attention to the compartment.

"Someone might look in," Christine said.

"Who might?"

"Anybody going by."

"The whole train is asleep."

"Or if we stop at a station . . ."

"No scheduled stops. You know we've been rerouted."

It reminded her of the joke about Lenin saying, "Stop worrying, the train's sealed!" She wondered if this was a good time to tell it.

Herbert said, "Now that we're alone, tell me something."

"What?"

"Isn't it a bit of a pose, your reading? Why did you say you were reading for an exam?"

"I didn't say it was my exam," she said.

"You said that it was in two days' time."

"Yes. Well, I imagine that will be for students of theology who have failed their year."

"Of course," said Herbert. "That accounts for the Bonhoeffer. Well. Our Little Christian. What good does it do him if *you* read?"

"It may do me good, and what is good for me is good for both of you. Isn't that so?" For the second time that day her vision was shaken by tears.

"Chris."

"I do love you," she said. "But there has been too much interference."

"What, poor little Bert?" No, she had not meant interference of that kind. "You mean from *him*, then?" Sometimes Herbert tried to find out how much she lied to her official fiancé and whether she felt the least guilt. "What did you tell him about Paris?" he said.

"Nothing. It's got nothing to do with him."

"Does he think you love him?" said Herbert, blotting up her tears as though she were little Bert.

"I think that I could live with him," said Christine. "Perhaps there is more to living than what I have with you." She was annoyed because he was doing exactly what her fiancé always did – veering off into talk and analysis.

"It is easy to love two people at once," said Herbert, more sure of her than ever now. "But it can be a habit, a pattern of living; before it becomes too much a habit you ought to choose." He had seen the theology student and did not take him seriously as a rival. She glanced out to the empty corridor. "Don't look there," said Herbert.

"What if we are arrested?"

Perhaps he would not mind. Perhaps he saw himself the subject of a sensational case, baying out in a police court the social criticism he saved up to send to newspapers. She remembered the elaborate lies and stories she had needed for the week in Paris and wondered if they were part of the pattern he had mentioned. Suddenly Herbert begged her to marry him – tomorrow, today. He would put little Bert in boarding school; he could not live without her; there would never again be interference. Herbert did not hear what he was saying and his words did not come back to him, not even as an echo. He did not forget the promise; he had not heard it. Seconds later it was as if nothing had been said. The corridor was empty, and outside were the same plain of dried grass and the blind, hot, grey stucco box-houses they had been seeing all afternoon. She felt angry with Herbert, hateful even, because he had an unfailing hold on her and used it.

She said, "Herbert, that Norwegian is not interested in me; he is interested in you. And you know it."

Herbert accepted the accusation as though he were used to every kind of homage. He was tall, intelligent, brave and good-looking. He was generous and truthful. A good parent, a loyal friend. Never bore grudges. His family was worthy of him, on both sides. His distinguished officer father had performed his duty, nothing worse; his mother had defended her faith to the extreme limit. He was thirty-one and had made only one error in a lifetime: he had married a girl who ran away. He sat still and did not protest uselessly or say, "Unhealthy imagination. Projecting your own morbid desires. Insane jealousy," though he may have been thinking it. He accepted the Norwegian as a compliment.

She plunged on recklessly, just as she had kept the window open when there could have been fires, and said, "If it's men you want, you needn't think I am going to be a screen for you." He turned slightly and said, "Only one thing matters now – this train, which is running all over the map."

She did not wish to lose him. She *was* afraid of choosing – that was true – and she was not certain about little Bert. When he kept his head turned the other way, she quickly told the story about Lenin. He smiled, no more. There was a way out of their last exchange, but where? She had tried telling her joke with a Russian accent, but of course it didn't come off. She knew nothing about him. One thing she had noticed: when he had to speak on the telephone sometimes he would say "Berlin speaking," like a television announcer, or imitate some political figure, or talk broad Bavarian, which he did well, but it took seconds to get the real conversation moving, which was strange for a man as busy and practical as Herbert. She looked round for a change of subject – the landscape was hopeless – and said, "These seats aren't reserved. Why not move our things here?"

"No point, we've nearly arrived," said Herbert, and he opened the door and walked out, as if there were no reason for their being alone now. He strode along the rattling corridor with Christine behind him.

Interference came out to meet her halfway:

During the conflict we were enemy aliens. Went to be registered in a post office with spit all over the floor. From there to the police. Just as dirty. The jails must be really something once you're in them. Police had orders, had to tell us we couldn't go to the beaches any more. Big joke on them – we never went anyway, didn't even own bathing suits! Were given our territorial limits: could go into Jackson Heights as far as the corner of Northern and 81st. Never went, never wanted to. We could take the train from Woodside to Corona, or from Woodside to Rego Park, we had the choice, and ride back and forth as much as we liked. Never did, never cared to. We could walk as far as Mount Zion Cemetery but never did – didn't know anyone in it. Could ride the subway from Woodside to Junction Boulevard and back as much as we wanted, or Rego Park to 65th and back. Never did it once that I remember. The men could take the train to Flushing, they still worked at the same place, closely watched to see they didn't sabotage the submarine galley units. They had three stations from home to work, were warned not to get off at the wrong one. They never did. The thing was we never wanted to go anywhere except the three blocks between our two homes. The only thing we missed was the fresh bratwurst. We never went anywhere because we never wanted to! The joke was on the whole USA!

They were a happy party in the compartment now. Herbert seemed to feel he had put something over on the universe, and Christine felt she had an edge on both the Norwegian and little Bert. The other three were feeling splendid because they had slept. All were filled with optimism and energy, as if it were early morning. The Norwegian in particular was lively and refreshed and extremely talkative. Inevitably, being a foreigner, he began to do what Herbert called "opening up the dossier."

"On the subject of German reparations I remain open-minded," the Norwegian said amiably. "Some accepted the money and invested it, some refused even to apply. I knew of a lawyer whose entire career consisted of handling reparations cases, from the time he left law school until he retired after a heart attack."

"I am open-minded too," said Herbert, every bit as amiable as the Norwegian.

The woman in the corner spoke up: "What I keep asking myself is where does the money come from?" She looked at

Herbert, as if he should know. "And these payments go on! And on! Where does it all come from?"

"Don't worry," said Herbert. "The beneficiaries die younger than most other people. They die early for their age groups. Actuarial studies are reassuring on that point."

It was impossible for the two strangers to tell if Herbert was glad or sorry.

"It is only right that you pay," said the Norwegian, though not aggressively.

"Of course it is right," said Herbert, smiling. "However, I object to your use of 'you.'"

At this the conversation ran out. Christine removed herself from what might have been her share of feeling by opening her book. Instantly little Bert was beside her. "Read," he said.

She read, "'Bruno lived in a house of his own. He had a bedroom, a living room, a dining room . . .'"

"And a playroom."

"All right. 'The living room had red curtains, the bedroom had blue curtains . . .'"

"No," said little Bert. "Red in the playroom."

Herbert looked at them both; across his face was written, "It's working. They're friends." The woman in the corner had closed her eyes after the abrupt ending of the last conversation, but her mind was awake. *The other couple bought a car when the neighbourhood went. The three blocks weren't safe, they thought. Sometimes they were late for dinner because someone had parked in front of their garage. Otherwise they were always on time. At first they came just for lunch on Sundays, then got in the habit of staying for supper because Jack Benny came on at seven. The only words my sister-in-law ever learned in English were "Jello again." Once learned, never forgotten. Before the blacks came we had the Catholics. That was the way it went. Once I was waiting with my sister-in-law to cross the street in front of the house when a lot of little girls in First Communion dresses crossed without waiting for the light. So near you could touch them. I said to her, "You've got to admit they look nice in the white, like little snow fairies." One of those little girls turned right around and said in German, "We're not snow fairies, you old sow, we're angels – ANGELS!"*

Their train slowed at an unknown station, then changed its mind and picked up speed, but not before they'd been given a chance to see a detachment of conscripts of the army of the Federal Republic in their crumpled uniforms and dusty boots and with their long hair hanging in strings. She saw them as she imagined Herbert must be seeing them: small, round-shouldered, rather dark. Blond, blue-eyed genes were on the wane in Europe.

Herbert's expression gradually changed to one of brooding. He seemed to be dwelling on a deep inner hurt. His eyes narrowed, as if he had been cornered by beams of electric light. Christine knew that he felt intense disgust for men-at-arms in general, but for untidy soldiers in particular. His pacifism was certainly real – little Bert was not allowed to have any military toys. His look may have meant that even to a pacifist soldiers are supposed to seem like soldiers; they should salute smartly, stare you frankly in the face, keep their shoes shined and their hair trimmed. The Norwegian turned his mouth down, as though soldiering were very different where he came from. He exchanged a glance with Herbert – it was the first that Herbert returned. The woman in the corner opened her little eyes, shook her head, and said "Chck chck," marvelling that such spectacles were allowed.

The principal of Carol Ann's school had good ideas for raising money. One was the sale of crosses for one ninety-eight. Black crosses with the words HE DIED FOR YOU in white. Meant to be hung on a bedroom wall, the first thing a child would see in the morning. Character building. First of all my cousin did not want any cross in the house. Then he said he wouldn't mind having just the one so long as nobody said "crucifix." He couldn't stand that word – too Catholic. Then his wife said she didn't want a black cross because the black didn't match anything in the room. Everything in Carol Ann's bedroom was powder-blue and white. My cousin then said he did not want to see a cross with any person on it. Once you accept a cross with a person on it, they're in, he said, meaning the Catholics. My cousin was stricter than your average Lutheran. His wife said what about a white cross with powder-blue lettering? My cousin was really worked up; he said, "Over my dead body will a black cross called a crucifix and with any person on it enter my home." Finally Carol Ann got a white cross with no person on it and no words to read. It cost a little more, two forty-nine, on account of the white paint. The principal of that school had good ideas but went too far sometimes, though his aim was just to make people better Christians. The school earned quite a lot on the sale of the crosses, which went towards buying a dishwasher cut-rate from the Flushing factory. All the children were good Christians and the principal strove to make some better.

They were all tired now and beginning to look despondent. Luckily the next station stop was a pretty one, with gingerbread buildings and baskets of petunias hanging everywhere. The woman stirred and smiled to herself, as if reminded of all the charming places she had ever lived in during the past. The Norwegian leaped to his feet. "Good luck," said Herbert. He had given up trying to find water, toilets, food.

My cousin-in-law never understood the television. She'd say, "Are they the good ones or the bad ones?" We'd say this one's bad, that one's good. She would say, "Then why are they dressed the same way?" If the bad and the good had the same kind of suits on she couldn't follow.

"Read something about Bruno," said little Bert. "Read about Bruno not doing as he's told."

"'The fact was that Bruno could not always tell right from wrong,'" read Christine severely. "'When he was in Paris he whistled and called to other people's dogs. He did not know that it is not polite to call other people's dogs, even in a friendly way. He ate everything with his fingers. He put his fingers in the pickle jar.'"

"Careful. Our housekeeper does that," said Herbert.

"Read about Bruno's sisters and brothers," said little Bert. "What did *they* do?"

"'Bruno had five brothers. All five were named Georg. But Georg was pronounced five different ways in the family, so there was no mistake. They were called the Yursh, the Shorsh, the Goysh . . .'"

"Christine, *please*," said Herbert. "It's silly. The child is not an idiot."

"But, Herbert, it happens to be true! All five brothers had five different godfathers named Georg, so they were each called Georg. Is there a law against it?"

He searched and said, "No."

"Well then. 'The Goysh, the Jairsh . . .'"

"Don't confuse him," said Herbert.

"Oh, God, Herbert, you are the one confused. My father knew them. They existed. Only one survived the war, the Yursh. He was already old when I met him. He might be dead now."

"Well, all that is confusing for children," said Herbert.

"You're not reading," little Bert complained, but just then the Norwegian came back carrying an ice cream cone. Little Bert took it without saying thank you and at once began eating in the most disgusting manner, licking up the melting edges, pushing the ice down inside the cone, and biting off the end.

"Herbert," said Christine. "Please make him stop. Make him eat properly."

"Eat properly," said Herbert, smiling.

Conscious of so many adult eyes on him, little Bert began to lark about with the ice cream and make a fool of himself, at which everyone except Herbert looked the other way.

There was a plan to save some German cities, those with interesting old monuments. The plan was to put Jews in the attics of all the houses. The Allies would never have dropped a bomb. What a difference it might have made. Later we learned this plan had been sabotaged by the President of the USA. Too bad. It could have saved many famous old statues and quite a few lives.

"Now, little Bert," said Herbert, trying to clean the child's sticky face with a handkerchief, "we shall be leaving this train about two minutes from now. Another nice train will then take us to a place called Pegnitz. Pegnitz is a railway junction. This means that from Pegnitz there are any number of trains to take us home."

Little Bert could not have been listening carefully, for he said, "Are we home now?"

"No, but it is almost like being home, because we know where we're going."

"That's not the same as being home," said little Bert. He turned swiftly from Herbert and his eyes grew wide and amazed as the pregnant army wife, holding a wall for support, moved past their door. He looked at Christine and opened his mouth, but before he could ask anything loud and embarrassing, their conductor came in with new information: they must not wander too far away from the station during the stopover. They would soon see that they were just a few feet from a barbed-wire frontier, where someone had been shot to death only a week ago. They must pay close attention to signs and warnings concerning hostile police guards, guns, soldiers, dogs, land mines. Although this was good mushroom country, it was not really safe. Someone had been blown up not long ago while reaching for *Cantharellus cibarius*. The train to Pegnitz would be an unscheduled emergency transport for stranded passengers (theirs was not the only train to have been diverted), and this new transport might turn up at any moment. They were not to worry about their luggage: the conductor would look after everything. The train might arrive at any time, either five minutes or half an hour from now. All danger from the fires was over, the jolly conductor added. His hair was as shiny as leather and he bounded from one foot to the other as he gave the good news.

Herbert took down the woman's suitcase. She stuffed all her plastic bags and leftover food into the WINES OF GERMANY carryall. *I came back to Germany to bury my poor husband and look after his grave. Very rare for me to miss a day at the grave. I had to go and see about some investments. Otherwise I'm at the grave every morning with a watering can.*

As they shuffled along the corridor Herbert told Christine that he had folded and sealed his imaginary letter of protest about the train and was mailing it in his head to papers in Frankfurt, Hamburg, West Berlin, Munich, and Bonn; to three picture magazines, a trade journal, an engineering review, a powerful newsweekly and a famous TV commentator – but not to any part of the opposition press. He wanted to throw rocks at official bungling, but the same rocks must not strike the elected government. His letter mentioned high-handedness, lives disrupted without thought or care, blind obedience to obsolete orders, pig-headed officials, buck-passing, locked toilets, shortage of drinking water, absence of someone responsible, danger to health, indifference to others. Among the victims he mentioned a small child, an old woman, a visiting foreigner who would be left with a poor impression, a pregnant American, and a tall girl who wore nothing but size-eleven sandals and a short linen frock, who was travelling almost naked, in fact.

Hand in hand, perhaps wanting to avoid further instructions, Christine and little Bert made for the barbed wire they had been told to avoid. They walked along a sandy road that was strewn with candy wrappers, cigarette butts, bottle caps, and bent straws, like any sightseers' road anywhere. Little

Bert's hand felt as soft as the sand underfoot and as grubby as the rubbish on it. His natural surroundings were rust, wires, rain-washed warnings, sweet melting foods.

"Your father is getting you something to drink," she said, though he had not complained of thirst or of anything, and seemed content with promises. She showed him frontier posts looped with rusted wire like birthday ribbons. "You can die of tetanus if you catch your hand on it," she said. They stood on a height of land from which she could see two little villages flanking a smoking factory and a few scattered farmhouses with their windows boarded up on one side. No one in those houses could lean on the sill and observe little Bert, or Christine, or the barefooted old woman cutting grass for rabbits right to the first strands of rust, or a couple moving along at a crouch because they were hunting for mushrooms. Stern cautions against doing this had been nailed here and there, but people were used to these by now.

Little Bert began to play at hopping off the path. "You may step off one side, but not the other," she warned him. He no more questioned this than he had the meaning of tetanus. He appeared to have an inborn knowledge of what the frontier was about.

He was bored, however. "What are you looking at?" he said, with a return of his Paris whine. Being small he could not see farther than the first barrier. She counted off for him a fence, a tract of low scrub, fence again, scrub, more fence, deep-ditch trap, fence, trap again probably, fences clean and bright in the sun as they moved farther east. Shading her eyes, she found herself looking at a man in uniform who was looking at her through field glasses. He looked at her and at little Bert, who was tugging her hand and wailing, "Let's walk."

The child's bratty voice made another man turn; he was a civilian with a scarred hairline, strolling along the sandy road too with his hands behind his back. He seemed to measure everything he gazed on – seemed to estimate, memorize, and add to a sum of previous knowledge. He knew about the smoking factory on the other side and about its parasite villages; he remembered when there had been the rumour, years ago, that the factory, with its technicians and engineers, was to be dismantled and moved. No one had told him so: he was too little then to be trusted. He knew something had frightened the adults; he could read their mute predictions. All bicycles had been confiscated, even the children's. He had walked up the main street to the top of his village, which was shabby and countrylike. You could still find milk and an egg sometimes if you were not an informer. There he saw Marie sitting on a wheelbarrow, with her hair cut like a boy's (lice were rampant), blond and ragged; she was eating bread – or rather, sucking on a wide crust spread with boiled rhubarb. Bare dirty feet, eyes in the distance, dreamy: he thought later that he had seen clouds on her eyes, like clouds on a clean sky. But perhaps all that her eyes had reflected was stupidity. She swung her feet, which did not reach the ground because of the tilt of the barrow. The geese Marie was there to watch watched Sigi approaching with pure blue eyes outlined in orange that could have been drawn with a wax crayon, so thick was the tracing and the colour so true. The geese looked at him with one eye at a time, the way the Ancient Egyptians looked at people. His mother caught up with him before he could say anything final to Marie, either "I love you" or "Goodbye." He had been told not to play with Marie and to keep away from that part of the village – he had been told again only this morning. His mother was looking for milk. She hid the canister in a basket, under a napkin camouflaged with the wild sorrel and plantain they ate as vegetables now.

Sigi left Marie still pensive, still occupied with her bread-crust. He walked with his hand in his mother's. His mother said, "Did the Marie ask you any questions?" But Marie hardly ever spoke. His mother said that minding geese was too big a job for a little child; a long prison sentence was the punishment now for misappropriation of domestic fowl.

He was prepared for the end, perhaps the end of everything living, and he knew that endings were in blood. He decided to take to his execution *Peoples of the World*, a schoolprize of his father's, which was in perfect condition; his father never smudged or creased anything he owned and washed his hands before taking down a book. In this book were the Ancient Egyptians looking with one eye at a time precisely like Marie's geese. He closed his eyes so that his last memory would be of Marie.

"Why are you walking with your eyes shut?" asked his mother.

"I'm pretending to be blind."

"God will strike you blind if you play such wicked games." Normally she would have gone on to say exactly why God would want to do a thing like that. Her abrupt silence was part of the end of everything.

When she woke him up that night and dressed him (he could dress himself) she was still tongue-tied, and when *he* asked something she put her hand on his mouth.

"Tape it?" said his father, of Sigi's mouth. She shook her head. "God help us if you don't keep it shut, Sigi," said his father, bringing Him into it again. After he was dressed they gave him a glass of milk and told him to drink all of it. But they could not wait for him to finish drinking and when he was only halfway through his father removed the glass. His parents wore heavy coats and carried knapsacks. Sigi took *Peoples of the World* from under his pillow.

"No, you will need both hands," his father said. He pinched Sigi's arm, like the witch testing Hansel, and asked, "Will he be warm enough?"

The signs of the end of the world were being dressed in the night, the milky glass left on the table, and his mother's silence. She did not even ask why he had taken *Peoples of the World* to bed. Much later he fell asleep again. His father was carrying him, and woke him suddenly by setting him on his feet in a ploughed field. Unable to move, paralyzed, he heard a strange man cursing him, and suddenly his mother cried from another corner of darkness, "Run!" So he plunged at a crouch between ropes of barbed wire as if he had been trained for this all his life. The man cursing him for his slowness grabbed Sigi and dragged him face down. He looked up to see who it was and left a piece of his scalp on a wire. No matter how he combed his hair ever after the scar reappeared.

They went to live in Essen. He hated the food, school, traffic, accents, streets. No grass, no air to breathe. He would say to himself, "When I turn *this* corner, Marie will be here." Years later somebody sent a long letter with news of the village. Part of it was, "As for the Marie, she is so fat and stupid she falls off her bicycle."

"Some of them have bicycles," was all Sigi's father gleaned from this important letter.

His mother had kept a newspaper account of their adventure. He *knew* there had been just the three of them besides the unseen man who had cursed him, but the paper said they had been thirty-seven, the technical staff of the small lens factory and their wives and children.

He walked just in front of Christine and little Bert, holding a hand to his head because of the scar – a bad habit. He suddenly turned and came back so that they seemed to be walking towards a meeting point. She saw that he knew she knew everything; the expression on his face was one of infinite sorrow.

What are you doing here? she tried to ask as they nearly met. Why spend a vacation in a dead landscape? Why aren't you with all those others in Majorca and Bulgaria? Why bother to look? The houses are shuttered on one side. No one sees you except a policeman with field glasses. Marie wouldn't look even if she remembered you. Wouldn't, couldn't – she has forgotten how. Her face turns the other way now. Decide what the rest of your life is to be. Whatever you are now you might be forever, give or take a few conversions and lapses from faith. Besides, she said, as they silently passed each other, you know this was not the place. It must have been to the north.

Herbert had never seen such a hideous station or such a squalid town – so he said now, catching up to them. Prussian

taste, he said, and all Napoleon's fault. By what right did
Napoleon turn us over to the Prussians, he wanted to know? *En
quel honneur?* He sounded as though he might write a letter to
the newspapers complaining about Napoleon. He had discovered something curious, he went on: a coffeehouse on stilts.
Part of its attraction, other than a trio of musicians (fiddle,
accordion, xylophone) was the view it afforded of the ditches
and mantraps over there. From the coffeehouse veranda you
could even see a man in uniform looking through field glasses.
"You don't see that often," said Herbert, but he meant the
orchestra. He continued in French, for he did not want little
Bert to hear: the veranda on stilts was full of guest workers
talking Turkish, Croatian and North African dialects. Though
needed for the economy, the guest workers had brought with
them new strains of tuberculosis, syphilis, and amebic com-
plaints that resisted antibiotics. Everyone knew this, but the
government was hushing it up. Herbert had proof, in fact, but
he would not make it public, for he did not wish to favour the
opposition. But here was what he was getting at – Herbert did
not want little Bert, young and vulnerable, to drink out of the
same glasses as foreign disease-bearers. On the other hand,
he must not breathe the slightest whiff of racial animosity.
Therefore would Christine please engage the child's attention
until they had passed the coffeehouse?

They were moving back slowly, she holding little Bert's
hand, and he not fretting to be nearer his father, quite happy
with her. Presently they found they were four abreast with the
scarred stranger, all walking at the same pace. It would have
seemed awkward to have drawn back or hurried ahead. Just as,

shyly silent, they came level with the coffeehouse, the stranger spoke up: "That place is always packed with foreigners."

"What place?" said little Bert at once.

"Do you object to them?" said Herbert, in his most pleasant tone of voice.

"I don't know much about them. I never travel. My father was in Montenegro. The partisans gave him a bad time. I think I wasn't born yet. I'm not sure of the year. Forty-three?"

"I hope they gave him a bad time," said Herbert, who always said such things with a smile. People who did not know him had to think again, wondering what they had heard. No one knew how to deal with Herbert's ambiguities. "I hope they gave him a *very* bad time."

Could I have heard this? the scarred man seemed to appeal to Christine.

Suit yourself, she seemed to answer. I wasn't born either.

"Now the children of the partisans come here as guest workers," said Herbert, still smiling. "And we all drink coffee together. What could be better?"

The stranger edged away, went over to an old man standing by himself on the station platform and began to speak urgently in a low voice. The old man came up to his shoulder. He had not a tooth in his mouth, not a hair on his head, and was about the age and the size of the night porter in their Paris hotel. He was dressed in clean tennis shoes without laces, old army trousers, and a worn regional jacket over an open shirt. He rocked heel to toe as he listened, then said loudly to whatever it was the scarred man had asked, "I wouldn't know. I don't know any names around here. I'm a refugee too."

"His feelings are hurt," said Christine, as the stranger drifted away. "Look at the way he hangs his head. I'm sure he was asking a direction. Now, why did you answer that way?" she asked the old man. "I'm sure you are not a refugee at all. What didn't you like about the poor creature?"

"He's not from around here," said the old man. "He's from somewhere else, and that's enough for me."

"And you," she said to Herbert. "What didn't you like about him? Such a harmless lonely person."

He tightened his hold on her arm. "I saw the way he was watching you. Don't you know a policeman when you see one?"

She looked again, but the man had crossed the tracks and vanished. Anything he might have wanted to let her know was damped out by a stronger current; their companion with the WINES OF GERMANY shopping bag could not be far away. *On a hot day like today every plant on a grave can wither. Family spies on his side of the family inspect the grave, waiting for a leaf to fall or a flower to droop. But usually I'm right there with the watering can. He was fussy about the grave, often spoke of how he wanted it.*

"There isn't a restaurant," said Herbert, again in French. "It's hard on little Bert. Only a newsstand. I think on a day like today one might allow a comic book. Do you agree?"

But she was not the child's mother: she would not be drawn.

Herbert's answer to her silence was to march into the waiting room and across to a newsstand. She knew that by making an issue over something unimportant she had simply proved once again that wilful obstinacy was part and parcel of a slow-moving nature. She suffered from its effects as much as

Herbert did. Holding little Bert, she trailed along behind him, thinking that she would show her affection for Herbert now by being particularly nice to little Bert.

Herbert waited for the curator of the local museum to be served before choosing the mildest of the comic books on display. The curator walked off, reading the local paper as he walked. A ferocious war of opinion took up three of its pages. Was it about the barbed wire? About the careless rerouting of trains that had stranded dozens of passengers in this lamentable, godforsaken, Prussian-looking town? No, it was about an exhibition of photographs Dr. Ischias had commissioned and sponsored for his new museum – an edifice so bold in conception and structure that it was known throughout the region as "the teacup with mumps." Dr. Ischias was used to Philistine aggression; indeed, he secretly felt that his job depended to some extent upon the frequency and stridency of the attacks. But it seemed to him now that some of the letters in today's paper might have been written a good fifty years in the past. This time he was accused not just of taking the public for dimwits, but also of sapping morals and contributing to the artistic decline of a race.

"Once again" (he now read, walking out of the waiting room, holding the paper to his nose) "art has not known how to toe the mark or draw the line. Can filth be art? If so, let us do without it. Let us do without the photographer in question and his archangel, the curator with the funny name."

Well . . . that was unpleasant. Perhaps the show had been a mistake. It happened that the photographer in question had reproduced every inch of a model he said was his wife; in fact,

the exhibition was entitled "Marriage." These pictures had
been blown up and cropped so peculiarly that only an abstract,
grainy surface remained. As the newspaper had to admit, most
adults honestly did not know what the pictures were about.
However, most children, with their instinctive innocence,
never failed to recognize that this or that form was really part
of something else, which they named quite eagerly. And the
local paper did not tiptoe round the matter, but asked, in a
four-column double head on page two:

ARE GERMAN WOMEN BABOONS
AND MUST THEY ALWAYS EXHIBIT THEIR BACKSIDES?

This was followed up by a cartoon drawing of a creature, a
gorilla probably, with his head under the dark hood of an
old-fashioned camera on a tripod, about to take the picture of
three Graces, or three Rhine maidens, or three stout local
matrons who had somehow lost their clothes.

Now all this was libel – every word, and the drawing too.
The curator folded his copy of the paper and began to walk up
and down the platform, composing an answer.

Christine knew that Herbert could have helped him,
because he was good at that kind of letter, taking a droll, dry
tone, ending with, "Of course I am prepared to withdraw my
allegations at any time," mockingly humble. His letters
always drew a deluge of new correspondence, praising and
honouring Doctor Engineer Herbert B. But the curator did
not know that Doctor Engineer Herbert B. was just behind
him; in any case he was not doing badly with his own reply:

"A ray of light has just as much chance of penetrating into the thick swamp of the German middle-class mind as . . ." He clasped and unclasped his hands, the newspaper tucked high under one arm. "The myth of German womanhood, a myth belied every day . . ." Walking up and down the platform near the sandy road, seen by the man in uniform looking through field glasses. "As for the photographer in question, his international status places him above . . ." "Only the small-minded could possibly . . ." "People who never set foot in museums until drawn by the promise of pornography can hardly judge . . ." "Only children should be allowed into art galleries . . ." Excellent. That had never been said.

Meanwhile the photographer had descended from a local train and started to tell a story about grass fires. He was wearing his tartan waistcoat with George-the-Fourth buttons, his cream corduroy jacket from Rome, his cream silk turtleneck sweater, an American peace emblem on a chain, dark-green shorts, Japanese sandals, and, because the sandals pinched, a pair of brown socks. His legs were tanned and covered with blond fur. Although slim and fit, he seemed older than usual. This was on account of his teeth. He had recently acquired two new bridges, upper and lower, which took years off his face but were a torture, so today he had changed back to the earlier set. The dentist had told the photographer's wife, "His jaw is underdeveloped, like a child's, difficult to fit."

And she answered, "Yes, I see. Classic, aesthetic – no?"

"Well, jaws are always classical," said the dentist.

The photographer wanted to look a bit younger for the sake of his wife. Every season the difference in time between them seemed to increase. Most young wives of middle-aged men bridged the gap by looking older, but his wife grew more and more childlike. On their honeymoon in Florence he had shown her the marble likeness of a total stranger, saying, "There, the ideal – classic, aesthetic," and so forth; and she told her mother later and they had a good laugh. When the dentist made the remark about his jaws she saved it up for her mother too. Now the dentist had said he could make a third lot of teeth that would make the photographer appear to be twenty-eight and would not hurt as much as the last set, but the work would cost six hundred marks more.

As soon as he saw the photographer the curator began to shout everything he had just been thinking about the newspaper. The very sight of the photographer with his collapsed face and brown socks made the curator feel tense. He had to defend art as far as the first row of barbed wire, but he would have preferred doing this without ever meeting an artist, for they took up time. The curator's angry voice carried along the platform to the waiting room, where a cultural travelling group, tossed up between trains like Christine and the others, sat hungry and miserable with their cultural group leader. These people distinctly heard the curator say that he was opposed to womanhood. They put their heads together and began to whisper.

The group were on their way to the opera and had dressed for a cultural evening in July – that is, the men in white dinner jackets and the women with long skirts, and fur stoles they hugged around themselves in spite of the heat. They knew pretty well what the curator was yelling about because the most revolting of the photographs had been shown on television and in the picture magazines, and had been discussed in a syndicated editorial of the opposition press. The result was that this little frontier town, with its teacup-with-mumps museum, its reputation for pornography, and its forward-looking curator, was quite famous now. Most members of the group had actually heard the curator mouthing cultural insults in their own living rooms, with the colour TV lending a strange mauve tinge to his ears and chin. The photographer had scarcely been interviewed at all. He had nothing in the way of a social theory; he could only bleat that he loved his wife and thought marriage was noble and fulfilling. For some reason this irritated the public. He said nothing but simple and gentle things, yet everyone hated him and people had written letters to the government saying he ought to be lynched.

Now he walked along the platform with the curator in the boiling heat and said he had been wondering if the caricature of himself as a gorilla might not be just a little libellous. And the curator, sweating and cross, sick to death of art and artists, looked down at his legs and socks and snapped, "Oh, it's probably not libellous at all."

Little Bert stayed close to Christine and curled his hand tightly around her fingers. She remembered how he had wakened night after night in a strange room and found himself alone in the dark. At first he had not even known how the foreign light switch worked. She and Herbert had spoken French much of the time; no wonder the child had finally preferred to have conversation with a sponge.

"You'll soon be home," she said. "Are you hungry?"

The station buffet had run out of food and the newsstand
sold nothing to eat except cough drops and chewing gum.
Little Bert did not seem to notice; at least he did not say he
was hungry. He was only slightly interested in the comic book.
He was taking in the opera party, all in their sixties or so,
looking rather alike. They sat facing one another on two long
rows of benches, the women holding their fat knees together
under their long gowns. Perhaps these people did not know
each other well, except for their cultural meetings. There was
too much shy laughter, and too many Oh, do you think so's
after every remark. What they had in common at this moment
was their need of comfort; here they were, forced to change
trains, the new train late, and the women in particular having a
bad time of it, their makeup melting in the heat and having to
hear their sex and station in life criticized by the trumpet-
voiced curator. Luckily to console them they had their own
cultural group leader, a match for the curator any day.

The group leader, whose long chin all but hid his collar, and
whose eyes seemed startled and wise because his glasses mag-
nified them, sat with one hand on each knee, legs wide apart,
shoulders forward. It was not quite the position of a cultured
person, more the way a train conductor might perch between
rounds, but this might have been only because the bench was
so narrow. He spoke to them softly, looking from face to face,
and leaning left and right for those sharing his bench.

Within a few minutes he had wiped out of their memories
every vexation and discomfort they had been feeling. He
mentioned

Bach

Brahms

Mozart

Mahler

Wagner

Schubert

Goethe

Schiller

Luther and Luther's bible

Kant

Hegel

the Mann brothers, Thomas and Heinrich;
	true connoisseurs prefer the latter

Brecht – yes, Brecht

several Strausses

Schopenhauer

Gropius

and went on until he had mentioned perhaps one hundred familiar names. Just as everyone was beginning to feel pleasantly lulled, and even to feel oddly well fed, though a moment ago they had all been saying that they could eat the wooden benches, their leader suddenly said, "The Adolf-time . . ."

In the silence that followed he looked into every face, one after the other, sadly and accusingly, like a dog about to be left behind; the reproachful silence and sliding dog's glance went on for so long that one could have heard a thought. Christine did hear some, in fact: they were creaking thoughts, as old chairs creak. The whole cultural group held its breath and the thoughts creaked, "Oh, God, where is this kind of talk taking us?" Finally the cultural leader had to end his sentence because they could not go on holding their breath that way, especially those who were stout and easily winded. He concluded, ". . . was a sad time for art in this country."

Who could disagree? Certainly no cultivated person on his way to the opera. Yes, a sad time for art, though no one could remember much preoccupation with art at the time, rather more with coal and margarine. There had been no public exhibitions of women showing their private parts like baboons, if *that* was art. There had been none of that, said some of the creaking thoughts. Yet others creaked, "But stop! What does he mean when he says 'art'? For isn't music art too?" There had been concerts, hadn't there? And the Ring cycle, never before so rich and full of meaning, and *The Magic Flute*, with its mysterious trials, the Mass in B Minor, the various Passions, and the Ninth Symphony almost whenever you wanted it? There must have been architecture, sculpture, historical memoirs, bookbinding, splendid colour films. Plays, ballet – all that went on. Cranach, Dürer, the museums. Surely the cultural leader must have meant that it was a sad time *in general*, especially towards the end.

He was still speaking: "As I stood before the new opera house, the same house you are about to see – if our train ever does arrive –" (smiles and anxiety) "a distinguished foreigner said to me, 'If only you Germans had thought more about *that* . . .'" pointing as the distinguished foreigner had pointed, but really indicating a gap between two women sitting with their knees clenched. He continued, "'. . . instead of material things, it would have been better for you and for everybody . . .'"

Following this closely, Little Bert turned to where the man had pointed and saw nothing but the newsstand, which was not any kind of a house. Christine saw little Bert looking at a row of pornographic magazines, the sort that were sold everywhere now, and wanted to cover his eyes, but as Herbert had said, one could not protect him forever.

The cultural group exhaled, then breathed in deeply and gently. The women did something melancholy with the corners of their mouths. "As for the orchestras in those days," said the leader cheerfully, "they played like cows and they knew it. I remember how one execrable fiddle said to another, equally vile, 'Are you a Party member too?'"

This was a comic story – it must be. Their sad faces began to clear. All the same, no one was doing much more than breathing carefully in and out. Their creaking thoughts were scattered and lost as two new people, the Norwegian and the American army wife, appeared. The Norwegian greeted Herbert rather formally; the girl marched up to the newsstand, and after giving the rack of pornography a short, cool glance, indicated, somewhere beyond it, *Time*, *Life*, and *Newsweek*.

"They take their culture with them," said the Norwegian. "And what a culture it has become. Drugs, madness, sadism, poverty, lice, syphilis, and several other diseases believed to have died out in the Middle Ages."

"The girl is German," said Herbert, smiling.

"Oh, Herbert, no," said Christine. "Everything about her . . .
the hat . . . the shell necklace . . . everything . . . the hair. She
could not be anything but what she is."

"I agree," said Herbert. "German. Now, little Bert," he went
on, "do you see the train which is just arriving? It will take us to
Pegnitz. Once there we are almost home. Pegnitz is a junction.
Trains go through every few minutes, in all directions. In *most*
directions," he corrected.

Now that their transport was here a number of those who
had been grumbling at the delay suddenly decided that they
did not want this train after all; they would wait for the regular
service, or hire taxis, or send telegrams asking their relatives to
come and pick them up in cars. Finally, after a certain amount
of elbowing and jostling, only the hungry woman, the cultural
group going to the opera, the Norwegian, some German soldiers with hair like pirate wigs, the pregnant American girl,
and little Bert's party climbed aboard. This train was neat,
swept, cool; the first-class carriage was not crowded and had
plastic-leather seats. The opera party immediately spread out
and filled three compartments. The hungry woman, caught up
in the platoon of soldiers, disappeared, swept on to second
class. But she could not have been far away: *The arrangement
was we each got fifty percent of the estate under a separate property
agreement. He never thought I would survive him. All his plans
were for how he would dispose of my fifty percent once I had passed
on. His fifty percent was to be for himself and half of mine for him,
and half for the little movie star Shirley Bimbo. He never never
thought I'd be there after him. I had this diabetes, pneumonia three
times, around the change of life I got nervous and lost all my hair,*

had to do the cooking wearing a turban. Later I got a women's complaint, had the works out, better to get it over with. No wonder he never thought I could survive him. He left his fifty percent to the little lamb of God, Carol Ann. What the dumb bastard didn't know was that I would get my half plus sixty-seven percent of his half because we were married in Muggendorf under a completely different set of laws and we never took the citizenship. So think that over in your grave, Josef Schneider! He turned out to have more than anyone knew. There were the savings, the property, some home appliances, the TV and that – but what he had salted away besides was nobody's business. It's invested over here now. Safer.

This time they shared their compartment with the American girl, who buried her pretty nose in her magazines. There was nothing else for her to do; she could not understand what they were saying. The missing traveller drew nearer. *He asked to be cremated and the ashes brought to Muggendorf and buried. He left eight hundred dollars just for somebody to tend the plot. I signed a promise to look after the grave; the money's being held. If I keep the grave looking good for five years running I get the eight hundred dollars. Only one year to go. Always had said he wanted his ashes scattered on the trout stream at Muggendorf. Must have changed his mind. Just as well. Might be a fine for doing it. Pollution.* She saw them, perhaps had been looking for them and came in and sat down. As Herbert had said, it was as good as being home.

A woman we knew had this happen – her husband said he wanted his ashes flung to the winds from a dune by the North Sea. No planes in those days, had to take the ashes over by boat. Went up to Holstein, would climb on a dune, change her mind. Hated to part with poor Jobst. Noticed more and more barbed wire along the dunes, didn't know why. Never read the papers, had got out of the habit in the USA. Dreamed that Jobst appeared and said the world would experience a terrible catastrophe if she didn't scatter his ashes. Went back to the beach as near as she could to the sea, flung one handful east, one south, one west, was about to turn north when somebody grabbed her arm, two men with revolvers, the conflict had begun, they thought she was making signs to submarines.

They arrived at Pegnitz at dusk. Everyone began to shuffle along the corridor, peering out at the station they had been told was a junction. The train seemed becalmed in an infinity of tracks meeting, merging, and sliding away. Little Bert said to his sponge, "There are cows, one black, one brown, one dappled." But of course no cows were to be seen in the yard, only lights flashing and signal stations like sentry boxes. The woman sorted out the food she had left – biscuits, chocolates, grapes, oranges, macaroons, portions of cheese in thin silver paper – and placed everything in one clean plastic bag which she unfolded out of her purse, and on which was printed

CANARY BED

WARM, HYGIENIC, AGREEABLE

Above these words was the drawing of a canary tucked up in sheets and blankets for the night. *Shirley Bimbo, Shirley Bimbo,* she was telling herself.

All of them got to their feet too soon, as people do when they are tired of travelling. The train seemed to coast slowly and endlessly along a long platform. Christine stood between the Norwegian and little Bert, who put his nose on the window, making it white and button-shaped. When he glanced up at her he had two round patches of dirt, one on his forehead.

"Again," exclaimed the Norwegian.

"What?"

He did not mean little Bert. He was glaring at a detachment of conscripts lounging and sitting slumped on their luggage, yelling at one another and laughing foolishly. Christine said, "They are only farmers' sons who have been drafted, you know. Poor lads who have never studied anything. Boys like that must exist everywhere, even where you come from." But then she remembered how kind he had been to little Bert, and how generous about singing. She tried to agree with him: "I must say, they aren't *attractive*. They do seem to be little and ugly." She paused. "It's not their fault."

"They always looked that way," said the Norwegian. "They were always very little and very ugly, but they frightened us."

Christine had none of Herbert's amiable ambiguities. She said sadly, "We don't even know each other's names."

He pinched his nostrils and did a few seconds' puffing without making a reply. The important part of the journey had ended, as far as he was concerned, because he had finally said what he thought.

Yet it isn't over, she said to herself. She saw threads, crystals, flying horizontally like driven snow, and she caught as clear as the summer night a new tone on a different channel: *Dear Ken   sorry I haven't written sooner but you know how it is Dear Ken   sorry I haven't written sooner but you know how it is*

"Now, be ready," called Herbert over his shoulder. He had seen their new train standing empty on the far side of the tracks. "Christine? Little Bert?" Little Bert clasped his sponge and was ready. Herbert opened a door on which was written "Do Not Open" and helped the other two down. But after making a run for it they found the carriages were dark and the doors locked, and that a sign hanging upside down said "Coburg-Pegnitz," which was more or less where they had come from. "You must never do this, little Bert," said Herbert.

"Never do what?"

"Open the wrong door and cross the tracks. You could be killed or arrested."

They made their way to the platform by lawful means, through an underpass. The station was crammed with passengers who had been turned out of a number of rerouted trains, shouting, arguing, complaining, and asking questions. The American girl stood gazing up at "Pegnitz" as if she could not believe what she saw. She seemed fragile and lonely.

"Help her," said Christine. "She doesn't understand. Herbert, you can speak English."

"*En quel honneur?*" said Herbert. "Her German is probably better than little Bert's."

Perhaps it was true, or else when she was among Germans she did not want to hear what they said. She had just returned from the square behind the station where the bus to Pottenstein was usually parked. But everything had been changed around; there wasn't even a schedule in sight, and everyone on the platform was trying to find out when some train would come by to take them away from Pegnitz. She was seven and a half months pregnant, she had been travelling for hours now, and her back ached. All at once she turned and looked at Herbert. He looked back – respectfully, she believed. She pushed her way over to him through the crowd on the platform and said in her haughtiest English, "Sir! Vare iss ze boss to Buttonshtah?" which was enough to tell any careful census taker (Herbert, for one) her nationality, schooling, region, village – what part of village, even, if one was particular over details.

The fact of the matter was that she was on her way home to Pottenstein and that her shape was bound to be something of a shock to her parents. However, once they had recovered consciousness they would certainly try to help. For instance, they had a friend, a garage mechanic who had worked for two years in America and knew the customs. He had returned to Pottenstein for two reasons: one, when Americans invited him to their houses they would offer him something to drink and never a bite to eat, which showed that they were not refined; and two, he had been offended by the anti-German tone of the television commercials for a certain brand of coffee. This man would be called in to look at the letter she had intercepted, stolen, read in secret, and reread until she could see every word with her eyes tight shut. He would tell her how to use the letter in order to further her case – providing she had a case at all.

Just as Christine understood all this from the beginning, just as information arrived in the form of an unwieldy package the colour of bricks, Herbert, with sober face, began to speak with the accent of their train conductor. He said she was not far from Buttonshtah, only a few miles. He believed there existed a bus service.

"I know, but vare iss ze boss?" she complained, before she remembered that she was not supposed to know any German, let alone German spoken with that accent. She had been deceived by the look of Herbert; he was nothing more than a local product like herself. "Country pipples," she said, and showed them what it was to walk off with your nose in the air. Christine caught again, faintly, *Dear Ken   sorry I haven't written sooner but you know how it is*

Herbert did not want to rub it in but he did say, "You know, an American could live fifty years in Pottenstein without knowing it was Buttonshtah."

The Norwegian still thought the girl might be an American. He said that perhaps she had mistaken the "P" of "Pegnitz" for the first letter of "Pottenstein," and been too disturbed to read the rest. But Herbert laughed and said no American would do that either.

By now Christine knew all this. Herbert, who knew nothing, had fixed upon the essence of it: the girl was ashamed of being thought German by other Germans.

Little Bert tugged at Christine, trying to tell her something. "Is there time?" she asked Herbert.

She saw him nod before a new wave of soldiers pushed him back. He'll write a letter about *that*, she thought. Little Bert was very good about standing in the queue outside the door marked "Ladies" and neither giggled nor stared once inside. She found it curious that he had asked her and not his father; it was certainly the first time. When they came out Herbert was nowhere in sight; there were twice as many people as before milling about and protesting, and they saw the cultural group, quite red in the face now, the women clutching their furs as if the inhabitants of Pegnitz were bandits. Their leader had lost his spectacles and was barely recognizable without them. His eyes were small and blue, and he looked insane.

"A short wait. In there," said the stationmaster, running past Christine with a long list of passengers' names in his hand.

"We can sit down for a few minutes," said Christine. "In any case, we could never find your father in this confusion." She saw a place on a bench and squeezed little Bert in beside her. Nearly every inch of bench was occupied by women carrying luggage tied with string. A window on the side opposite the platform gave onto the freight yards.

"Read to me," said little Bert.

She noticed that some of the women glanced at them with consternation, even disapproval. It was true that little Bert seemed spoiled and that his voice was often annoying to adults.

"I suppose we seem like a funny-looking pair," she said to him. "Both of us filthy, and you with your bath sponge."

"The ladies are funny too," he said.

The women sat grouped by nationality – Polish, French, Greek, Russian, Dutch. Her eyes caught on the Frenchwomen, who were thin and restless, with cheeks flushed either by rouge or tuberculosis, and hair swept up and forward and frizzed with tongs. They were almost uniformly dressed in navy-blue suits and white blouses, and their shoes had thick wooden soles. Their glance was hostile, bright and missed nothing.

But they are not dirty, she said to herself. No more than we are at this moment. I shall tell the truth about it, if I'm asked. Herbert hasn't washed or shaven since yesterday. He brushed his teeth at Stuttgart, nothing more. As for little Bert . . .

"Whatever happens," she said to little Bert swiftly, "we must not become separated. We must never leave each other. You must stop calling me 'the lady' when you speak to your father. Try to learn to say 'Christine.' "

The child sighed, as he did sometimes when Herbert took too long to explain. "Read," he said sleepily.

"I can't remember a thing about Bruno."

"Look in your book."

"My mind is a blank." Nevertheless she opened it near the beginning and read the first thing she came to: " 'Shame and remorse are generally mistaken for one another.' It's no good reading that." She leaned against the child and felt his comforting breath on her arm.

"What happens then?" said little Bert after a pause. "That's not what you were reading before."

Their familiar bun-faced conductor now made an appearance. "Oh, thank God," said Christine. "He'll know about the train." He had stopped just inside the door. He scowled at the waiting women and, being something of a comedian, did an excellent impersonation of someone throwing a silent tantrum. First he turned red and his eyes started, then all the colour left his face and he could not part his lips, could only gesticulate. It was extremely clever and funny. Little Bert applauded and laughed, which drew the conductor's attention. He walked over to them slowly with his thumbs in his belt and stopped a few inches away, rocking on his heels. Suddenly he prodded the bath sponge.

"What have you got there?" he asked. "Who said you could have it?"

"Don't use that tone with the child," said Christine. "Children don't always understand games."

"Yes, I do," protested little Bert.

She was surprised to feel the panic – stronger than mere disapproval – that the other women were signalling now. She wondered if they weren't simply *pretending* to take fright. It was so evident that he had no power! Why, even the little girls from the summer camp had not been taken in.

He retreated a step – to lend the distance authority required, perhaps – and cried, "Who told you to come here?"

"Please lower your voice," she said. "We aren't playing. We have every right to sit where we choose, and the child has a right to his toy."

"Sponge," said little Bert. "Not toy."

The conductor leaned over them, his face so near that she could see specks of gold in his brown eyes. He said, "You won't say bad things about me, will you?"

"To the stationmaster? I'm not sure."

"No, to anyone. If anyone asks."

"You were rude a moment ago," she reminded him.

"But I was kind on the train. I let you keep the window open when we went through the fire zone." True enough, but had he really been *kind*? "You'll testify for me, then?" he said. "If you are asked?"

"What about these passengers?" she said, meaning the other women. "You were making faces – scaring them. They're still frightened." Indeed, some of them looked positively ill with terror. However, now that Christine had shown him up he was unlikely to begin playing again; the game would have no point. "Perhaps you would like to find out about our train?" she said. "The child is quite tired."

He waddled away, either because he was anxious to show he was still the harmless creature he had been on the train, or because she had alarmed him and he wanted to escape.

"Read, now," said little Bert. "What happens?"

"I don't know any more."

"It's in your book," he said.

Dear Ken   sorry I haven't written sooner but you know how it is The girl was still searching for the bus to Pottenstein. Or perhaps she had given it up, couldn't face the family, knew the letter was hopeless as evidence. It was faint and faded now – committed to a dull mind, to no real purpose. A mush like a mixture of snow and ashes surrounded the information. *I suppose several people figure I squared up on you   I don't think you thought that   I came to within a hair of getting busted and for all practical purposes I did get busted   when I got to the airport I was still tripppping*

I went to the restroom to change   I didn't have a poplin shirt or a tie   it took me a long time to get myself together

I looked like something from woodstock with a uniform on   do you remember the guy in munich who tried to get us to go to his car   well, I met him in the restroom   he had gotten scared about bringing it into the states so he was trying to get rid of it   he was in bad shape too   I processed out with him   as I was

"Why aren't you reading?" said little Bert. Only stubbornness still kept him awake.

"There's too much interference," she said. "I'm waiting for it to stop."

going through the customs line there were three guys ahead of me   they searched the first guy as if they thought he had a ton of smack   they asked him to empty his pockets

well, when I saw this the first thing I did was turn white, the second thing I did was fall out of line and look for a place to get rid of what I had on me   the room was full of people

I sat down on the convair belt that brought our bags into the room   there I took it out of my pockets and put it under the belt, never to see it again   I ran back and got in line

I was next by then   the guy took one look at me and knew I was scared to death   he went over me with a fine-tooth comb and I was never so glad not to have it on me in my life   we left there and went to ft dix   it was about 9:00 pm   they took our records and sent us to bed   next morning we got up cleaned the barracks and went on police call   after that we turned in to supply one set of greens, one poplin shirt, one overcoat, one field jacket   I didn't have any of this and it didn't matter   that's all you have to have and they don't care if you have it or not   after that you get a lot of crap about being a veteran, some of which is good to know   then you go and get paid and that's the last thing

after I was paid I took a cab to the airport. there I went to the rest room removed my uniform threw it in the trashcan, dressed went back up and got a ticket to Toledo where my mother lives   I stayed with her for two weeks trying to decide what I was going to do next   first I thought of sending you the 170 I owe you getting a job,

*but things were so screwed up there I had to leave or go crazy   you
will see what I mean when you get out   you won't believe it   it's like
being in a crazy house here and you are the only one sane*

so I left and came here the trip cost me about 150

*I've spent some money since I've been out here and I have about 42
now   I've been looking for a job every day I've been offered a lot of jobs
most of them are 80 or 90 a week clear   the reason I haven't taken
any of them is they don't pay enough   you draw 65 clear a week
drawing unemployment so working forty hours you only draw 15 more
a week*

*no one is giving the good jobs right now because the economy is
slow   the only thing I have to pay besides you is 12 a week to my sister
for staying here so I'll be sending you money every week until I get you
paid off   it really sucks living here with my sister and her
husband   he's a nice guy but he and my sister are really concerned
over me and they think I'm a great guy and when I'm here with them
they never leave me alone   they're great, it's just that they get on my
nerves   you'll understand this better once you get out*

when you come over we could take a place together

*write and tell me if the junk you had was good or not and how you
all came out on it   don't bring any back with you – mail it   it's like
gold here   my other advice is get out of the army first and forget
about her. Once you're out she can't touch you   tell her you want to
find a job first*

*you're crazy if you do it any other way   tell her you can't support
a family till you're twenty-one (joke)   I hope we can get together
after you get out   answer this letter right away   tomorrow I'm
going to get some grass I'll send you some   good luck Ken   love PS
it's 80° and I'm going to the beach*

"Is it finished?" said little Bert.

"I suppose so. Though nothing is ever finished," said Christine. She had been disappointed by both the substance and quality of this information.

"You never finished a story," little Bert said.

"I realize that. I'm sorry." He did not reply; living with adults had accustomed him as much to apologies as to promises.

She was always running, Herbert complained suddenly. *She streaked off like a hare. I went after. She doubled back. I tripped and fell. There we were, together. She seemed confident and competent, and I thought she did not need to be looked after. I must have dozed off. She woke me quite roughly saying, "You are supposed to be awake and making decisions. You are the man. That's how I've always heard it was played." The day she left she cut a lock of the child's hair. It was flaxen then. She took it close to the roots along the hairline. Destructive. Careless. When she needed money she sent the lock back to me. I understood immediately, sent money to a post-office address which was all she gave me, and returned the lock as well. After long-distance dialling was installed in the remotest villages she took to calling me late at night, never from the same place twice. So she said. Other people paid, without knowing it. You could tell she had her hand around the mouthpiece. She would say a few words and laugh. I never knew what she wanted. One night I heard, "Do you still love me?" I thought for a long time, wanting to give her a complete answer. After a while I said, "Are you still there?" She called again late in the winter. I said, "The answer to your last question is yes." She hung up quietly. Then silence. She was twenty-six, would now be twenty-eight.*

This fell like dirty cinders. As information, it offered nothing except the fact that Herbert was not far from the waiting room. Perhaps it had no connection with him; in this particular game no one was allowed an unfair advantage. It was old and tarnished stuff which had come to her by error. Complete information concerning Herbert had certainly been caught by someone who had no use for it. It was like the Pottenstein letter – each person involved with it was now in a different place, moving steadily in a new direction. A day of indecision could make all the difference between silvery flakes and mud.

Little Bert yawned and pressed the sponge against his mouth. His muffled voice said, "Read!"

The trouble about the grave is that he's got family living around Muggendorf. My cousin-in-law tipped them off. They're watching the grave closely. At the first sign of drought, weeds, plant lice, cyclamen mites, leaf hoppers, thrips, borers, whiteflies, beetles feeding, they'll take colour photographs of the disaster and use them as evidence. Which would mean the end of the eight hundred dollars.

"What are we waiting for now?" said little Bert.

"For the conductor to tell us about our train. It is much cooler in here." She had been going to add, "and there is less interference," but that wasn't true. At least the other women were silent; ever since Christine had put the conductor in his place they seemed afraid of her too.

"Read," said little Bert. "You never finished anything."

"What do you want as a beginning this time?"

"Whatever it says."

"I did read you a bit of that," she said. "You didn't like it."

Last Sunday they happened to find one bare spot and they planted an ageratum. A reproach. What nobody understands is that it isn't usual to buy a plot for just a can of ashes. I would have kept them at home, but his will had one whole page of special instructions. What can you put on a plot that size? Not much bigger than a cat's grave and the stone takes up room. The begonias are choking the roses and vice versa.

Little Bert yawned again, even wider. "You'll soon be home," she said.

"What do we do when we get home?" He had been away for a whole week, plus this long day.

And yet they managed to find room for one ageratum. Only one year to go. Hang on, I keep telling myself. Hang on for the eight hundred dollars. Worth hanging on for. After that I'll be ready to go. Plot purchased and paid up. Nowhere near him.

"You're not reading," said little Bert.

She waited a few seconds longer, until the air was clear. Perhaps the silent women were attracting everything to themselves without being conscious of it. Then she distinctly heard Herbert saying, *"En quel honneur?"* It was loud, for him, and rather frantic. She guessed it must have been his response to a piece of irritating news – that there would be a long delay, for instance. She wondered if she and little Bert should go out to him; but the child was tired and once they had left the waiting room they would have to stand, perhaps for a long time. While she was wondering and weighing, as reluctant as ever to make up her mind, a great stir started up in the grey and wintry-looking freight yards they could see from the window. Lights blazed, voices bawled in dialect, a dog barked. As if they knew what this animation meant and had been waiting for it, the women picked up their parcels and filed out without haste and without looking back.

"No, you stay here," said Christine, holding little Bert, who had made a blind move forward. He looked at her, puzzled perhaps, but not really frightened. When the door had closed softly behind the last of them she felt a relief, as at the cessation of pain. She relaxed her grip on the child, as if he were someone she loved but was not afraid of losing.

"Read," said little Bert. "Look in the book."

"I'll read for a minute," she said. "Then we will have to do something else."

"What?"

"I don't know," she said. "Go out, or wait here. I'm sorry to be so uncertain." He sat as near to her as when the room had been full. She opened her book and saw, "'The knowledge of good and evil is therefore separation from God. Only against God can man know good and evil.' Well," she said, "no use going on with that. Don't be frightened, by the way," she told little Bert, who was not frightened of anything, though in Paris he had pretended to be afraid of the dark.

That was the end of it. He's in Muggendorf and I'm hanging on. When Carol Ann learned to pronounce "th" did that make her a better Christian? Perhaps it did. Perhaps it took just that one thing to make her a better Christian.

She had been hoping all day to have the last word, without interference. She held little Bert and said aloud, "Bruno had five brothers, all named Georg. But Georg was pronounced five different ways in the family, so there was no confusion. They were called the Goysh, the Yursh, the Shorsh . . ."

The Old Friends

■

Part of the plot of their friendship, the reason for it, is that the police commissioner has become an old bachelor now, and his life rests upon other lives. He rests upon people for whom he is not really responsible. Helena is by far the most important. She is important quite in herself, because anyone with television in this part of Germany knows her by sight. The waitress, just now, blushed with excitement when she recognized her, and ran to the kitchen to tell the others.

The commissioner and Helena have been friends forever. He cannot remember when or how they met, but if he were asked he would certainly say, "I have *always* known her." It must be true: look at how charming she is today – how she laughs and smiles, and gives him her time; oh, scarcely any, if the minutes are counted, but as much as he needs, enough. She is younger than the commissioner, but if she were to turn away, dismiss him, withdraw her life, he would be the orphan. Yes, he would be an orphan of fifty-three. It is the greatest possible anxiety he can imagine. But why should she? There is no quarrel between them. If ever there was, he has forgotten it. It was never put into words. He is like any policeman; he knows one meaning for every word. When, sometimes, he seems to have transgressed a private rule of hers, it is outside the limits of the words he knows, and he simply cannot see what he has done. She retreats. In a second, the friendship dissolves, and, without understanding why he deserves it, he is orphaned and alone.

When the weather suits her and she has nothing urgent to do, she lets him drive her to a garden restaurant on a height of land above Frankfurt. It is in a suburb of quiet houses – "like being in the mountains," he says. He sniffs the air, to demonstrate how pure it is. "But you really should come here at night," he says; for then the swimming pool in each of the gardens is lighted blue, green, ultramarine. The commissioner flew over in a helicopter once, and it looked . . . it was . . . it should have been photographed . . . or painted . . . if it had been painted . . . described by *Goethe*, he cries, it could not have been more . . .

"Tell us about Goethe," Helena interrupts, laughing.

She has brought her little boy along. The three of them sit at a table spread with a clean pink cloth. On a silver dish, and on still another pink cloth, this one embroidered, are wedges of chocolate cake, and mocha butter cakes, and Linzer torte, and meringue shells filled with whipped cream, sprinkled with pink, green, yellow sugar. The champagne in the silver bucket is for the commissioner and Helena.

There is no view from here, not even of swimming pools. They are walled in by flowering shrubs. It is a pity, he says, for if they could only see . . .

"Tell the child what all these flowers are called," Helena interrupts. But the commissioner does not know their names. He knows what roses or tulips are, but most flowers have names he has never *needed* to know. Flowers are pale mauve or yellow in spring, blue or yellow as summer wears on, and in the autumn orange, yellow, and red. On a hot autumn day, the garden seems picked out in bright wool, like a new carpet. The wine, the cakes, the thin silver vase of bitter-smelling blooms ("Nasturtiums," he suddenly cries out, slapping the table, remembering) attract all the wasps in the neighbourhood. He is afraid for Helena – imagine a sting on that white skin! He tries to cut a wasp in two with a knife, misses, captures another in the child's empty glass.

"The child needs men, you see," Helena goes on. "He needs men to tell him what things are. He is always with women."

Somewhere in her career she acquired this little boy. She does not say who the father is, but even when she was pregnant, enormous, the commissioner never asked. He treated the situation with great tact, as if she had a hideous allergy. It would have been a violation of their friendship to have pried. The rumour is that the father was an American, but not a common drunken one, an Occupation leftover – no, it was someone highly placed, worthy of her. The child is a good little boy, never troublesome. He eats his cakes with a teaspoon, and it is a wobbly performance. His fingers come into it sometimes; then he licks them. He scrapes up all the chocolate on his plate, because his mother dislikes the sight of wasted food.

"I mean it. Talk to him," Helena says. She may be teasing; but she could be serious, too.

"Child," says the obedient commissioner. "Do you know why champagne overflows when the cork is taken out of the bottle?"

"No, why?" says Helena, answering for her son.

The commissioner reflects, then says, "Because air got in the bottle."

"You see?" she tells the boy. "This is why you need men."

She is laughing, so she must be pleased. She is giving the commissioner her attention. On crumbs like these, her laughter, her attention, he thinks he can live forever. Even when she was no one, when she was a little actress who would travel miles by train, sitting up all night, for some minor, poorly paid job, he could live on what she gave him. She can be so amusing when she wants to be. She is from – he thinks – Silesia, but she can speak in any dialect, from any region. She recites for him now, for him alone, as if he mattered, Schiller's "The Glove" – first in Bavarian, then in Low Berlin, then like an East German at a radio audition, then in a Hessian accent like his own. He hears himself in her voice, and she gets no farther than "*Und wie er winkt mit dem Finger,*" because he is laughing so that he has a pain; he weeps with it. He has to cross his arms over his chest to contain the pain of his laughter. And all the while he knows she is entertaining *him* – as if he were paying her! He wipes his eyes, picks up his fork, and just as he is trying to describe the quality of the laughter ("like pleurisy, like a heart attack, like indigestion"), she says, "I can do a Yiddish accent from Silesia. I try to imagine my grandmother's voice. I must have heard it before she was killed."

She has left him; he is alone in the garden. He does not know the word for anything any more. He has forgotten how one says "hedge" or "wasp" or "nasturtium." He does not know the reason for the transparent yellow light in his glass. Everything assembled to please her has been a mistake: the flowers on the table smell too strong; the ice in the bucket is melting because the sun, too hot, is straight upon it; and the bottle of champagne, half empty, tipped to one side, afloat, is inadequate and vulgar. He looks at the red trace of the raspberry cake he had only just started to eat, at the small two-pronged fork, at the child's round chin – he daren't look at Helena. He discovers a crumb in his throat. He will choke to death, perhaps, but he is afraid to pick up his glass. Here he is now, a man in his fifties, "a serious person," he reminds himself, in a bright garden, unable to swallow a crumb.

She sits smoking, telling herself she doesn't need him – that is what he imagines. The commissioner is nothing to her, a waste of time. It is a wonder she sees him at all. He feels the garden going round and round, like the restaurant in Frankfurt that revolves on its hub. He would have taken her there often if she allowed it. He likes spending money on her, being reckless; and also, when he gives his card, the headwaiter and all the waiters know the commissioner and Helena are friends. But the restaurant is too high up; it makes her ill and giddy just to look out the window. And anyway she has enough publicity; she doesn't need to have a waiter bow and stare. What can he do for her? Nothing, and that is what makes her so careless – why she said the wounding thing just now that made him feel left out and alone.

Oh, that grandmother! That mother! She has a father somewhere, alive, but she shrugs when she mentions him, as if the living were of no use to her. The commissioner knows nothing about the mother and grandmother. He never met them. But he knows that where Helena was concerned a serious injustice was committed, a mistake; for, when she was scarcely older than the child at this table, she was dragged through transit camps on the fringes of Germany, without – thank God – arriving at her destination. He has gone over it so many times that her dossier is stamped on his mind, as if he had seen it, typed and signed, on cheap brownish wartime paper, in a folder tied with ribbon tape. To the dossier he adds: (One) She should never have been arrested. She was only a child. (Two) She is partly Jewish, but how much and which part – her fingers? Her hair? (Three) She should never have been sent out of the country to mingle with Poles, Slovaks, and so on. Anything might have happened to her. This was an error so grave that if the functionary who committed it were ever found and tried, the commissioner would testify against him. Yes, he would risk everything – his career, his pension, anonymous letters, just to say what he thinks: "A serious mistake was made." Meanwhile, she sits and smokes, thinking she doesn't need him, ready at any second to give him up.

The proportion of Jews in the population of West Germany is .04, and Helena, being something of a fraction herself (her fingers? her hair?), is popular, much loved, and greatly solicited. She is the pet, the kitten – *ours*. She wasted her lunchtime today on an interview for an English paper, for a special series on Jews in Germany. Through an interpreter (insisted upon by Helena; having everything said twice gives her time) she told a story that has long ago ceased to be personal, and then the gaunt female reporter turned her head and said, filtering her question through a microphone, "And was the child? . . . in these camps? . . . sexually? . . . molested?"

Rape is so important to these people, Helena has learned; it is the worst humiliation, the most hideous ordeal the Englishwoman can imagine. She is thinking of maniacs in parks, little children attacked on their way to the swimming pool. "Destruction" is meaningless, and in any case Helena is here, alive, with her hair brushed, and blue on her eyelids – not destroyed. But if the child was sexually molested, then we all know where we are. We will know that a camp was a terrible place to be, and that there are things Helena can never bring herself to tell.

Helena said, "It was forbidden."

The interviewer looked at her. Do you call that a bad experience, she seemed to be thinking. She turned off the tape recorder.

"Rape would have meant one was a person," Helena might have gone on to say. Or, "There wasn't that sort of contact." She has been wondering for years now exactly what it is they all want to hear. They want to know that it could not have been worse, but somehow it never seems bad enough. Only her friend, the commissioner, accepts at once that it was beyond his imagination, and that the knowledge can produce nothing more than a pain like the suffering of laughter – like pleurisy, like indigestion. He would like it to have been, somehow, not German. When she says that she was moved through transit camps on the edge of the old Germany, then he can say, "So, most of it was on foreign soil!" He wants to hear how hated the guards were when they were Slovak, or Ukrainian. The vast complex of camps in Silesia is on land that has become Polish now, so it is as if those camps had never been German at all. Each time she says a foreign place-name, he is forgiven, absolved. What does it matter to her? Reality was confounded long ago. She even invents her dreams. When she says she dreams of a camp exactly reproduced, no one ever says, "Are you sure?" Her true dream is of purification, of the river never profaned, from which she wakes astonished – for the real error was not that she was sent away but that she is here, in a garden, alive.

His failing, as a friend, is his memory. He thinks she has three birthdays a year, and that he has known her forever. They met

on a train, in Austria, between Vienna and Salzburg. He thinks
she was always famous, but he has forgotten that she was just
beginning, barely known, so anxiously dressed that sometimes
people thought she was a prostitute. They were alone in a
compartment. He sat with his hands on his knees, and she
remembers his large cufflinks and his large square ring. He was
like the economic miracle not yet at its climax of fat. Or he had
been obese a long time ago – she saw, around him, the ghost of a
padded man. He talked very seriously about the economic life of
every town they passed, as if he knew about it, but the one thing
she could recognize, whatever its disguise, was a policeman.

It makes her laugh now to think of the assurance with
which he asked his first questions: Are you married? What do
you do? Why were you in Vienna? She had been recording a
play for a broadcast. She was just beginning, and would travel
anywhere, overnight, never first class. She thought he had recognized her – that he had seen her, somewhere, once. The card
she gave him, with her name engraved, was new. He studied
the card for minutes, and ran his thumb over it absently.

"And in Salzburg you will be . . ."

"A tourist." To make the conversation move faster, and to
tease, to invent, to build a situation and bring it crashing down,
she said, "No one is expecting me."

"Are you expected anywhere?"

"Not until Monday. I live in Frankfurt."

He looked out the window for some time. He put the card
in his pocket and sat with the tips of his fingers pressed
together. "If no one is waiting for you," he said finally, "you
could skip Salzburg and come on to Munich with me. I have

some business there, so I would be busy part of the day. But I am free in the evening, and it is a very lively place. We could go to a night club. There is one like a stable; you drink in the horses' stalls. In the daytime, you could go to a museum. There is a very good museum where you can see ancient boats made out of hide, and you can see the oars. There are guided tours . . . The guide is excellent! And the station hotel is very good. If you don't want to, you needn't leave the station at all. Then we could both be in Frankfurt on Monday. I live there too. No one is meeting me. It wouldn't even matter if we were seen getting off the train together."

"What would happen if I went to Munich?" she said. "Would you give me money?"

"I? No."

"Well, no money, no Munich."

What went over his face was, Let me straighten this out. I thought you were one sort of person, but it seems you are another. What can this mean?

"Before I get down at Salzburg, I just have time to tell you a funny story," she said. "It is about paying for things. I heard it when I was a child, in a concentration camp." How tense they become, she thought. Just say two words and they stiffen, as if they had been touched with the point of a pin. "This is my story. A poor old Jew who was eating his lunch out of a piece of newspaper happened to be sitting opposite a Prussian officer in a train. The train was going to . . . to Breslau. After a time the officer said, 'Excuse me, but I want to ask you a question. What makes you Jews so clever, so that you always have the advantage over us?' 'Why, it is because we eat carp heads,' said the old man. 'And as I happen to have one here, I can sell it to you for thirty marks.' The officer paid for the fish head, and ate it with some disgust. After a time he said, 'But I have paid you thirty marks for something a fishmonger would have given me for nothing!' 'There, you see?' said the old man. 'It's working!'"

Her innocent eyes never left his face. He looked at her, so bewildered, so perplexed. What went wrong in our conversation, he seemed to be saying. Where was my mistake? Why are you telling me this old story? What have I done? He was red when he began to speak. His throat unlocked, and he said, "I never thought I should offer you money, Miss Helena. Excuse me. If I should have, then I apologize. You seem . . . a woman like you . . . so educated, so delicate . . . so refined, like a . . . *Holbein*." All this in his Hessian accent, which she was already recording, in her mind, for her own use.

If she were to remind him now about that man on the train, the commissioner would say, "What a fool! He could have been arrested." She imagines the commissioner arrested, still on the train, both hands against the pane and his face looking out between them – the anguish, the shock, as the train slid off and he wondered what he had done. "Now do you see?" she would say to him. "Now do you see what they are about – all those misunderstandings? You are that man too." But he would only know that another injustice had been committed; another terrible mistake.

In their conversations there is only one context. No remark is ever out of the blue. And so, when she leans forward, putting her cigarette out, at the table spread with a pink cloth, and says, "I was never raped," he does not look surprised. He says, "When you were in those places?"

"Yes. Rape did not occur. It was, in fact, utterly forbidden."

Putting out the cigarette she seems to lean on it. He knows only one thing, that the crisis is over. He has come through, without being wounded. Whatever the quarrel was, he is forgiven. They are here, with the child, in the garden restaurant, with the flowers like coloured wool. He is still the old bachelor in part of her life. Now he begins to understand what she has just said – the meaning of it. He would like to stand up and announce it, tap his fork on the wineglass and when he had everyone's attention say loudly, so that he could be heard all over the gardens and swimming pools, "Nothing like that happened – nothing at all. It was strictly, utterly forbidden!" He finds he can swallow – nothing, at first; just a contraction of the throat. Then he swallows a sip of his drink. He picks up his fork, bites a piece of raspberry cake, swallows. Tears stand in his eyes. She is the best friend he could ever have imagined. She has, again, brought him out of anxiety and confusion; he is not an orphan. When she lets the wasp escape from the glass he says nothing. He knows that a little later she will tell him why.

An Autobiography

■

I

I teach elementary botany to girls in a village half a day's journey by train from Montreux. Season by season our landscape is black on white, or green and blue, or, at the end of summer, olive and brown, with traces of snow on the mountains like scrubbed-out paint. The village is made up of concentric rings: a ring of hotels, a ring of chalets, another of private schools. Through the circles one straight street carries the tearooms and the sawmill and the stuccoed cinema with the minute screen on which they try to show things like *Ben-Hur*. Some of my pupils seem interested in what I have to say, but the most curious and alert are usually showing off. The dull girls, with their slow but capacious memories, are often a solace, a source of hope. Very often, after I have been on time for children raised to be unpunctual, or have counselled prudence, in vain, to these babies of heedless parents, I remind myself that they have not been sent here to listen to me. I must learn to become the substance their parents have paid for – a component of scenery, like a tree or a patch of grass. I must stop battering at the sand castles their parents have built. I might swear, at certain moments, that all the girls from Western Germany are lulled and spoiled, and all the French calculating, and the Italians insincere, and the English impermeable, and so on, and on; but that would be at the end of a winter's day when they have worn me out.

At the start of the new term, two girls from Frankfurt came to me. They giggled and pushed up the sleeves of their sweaters so that I could see the reddish bruises. "Tomorrow is medical inspection," said Liselotte. "What can we say?" They should have been in tears, but they were biting their lips to keep from laughing too much, wondering what my reaction would be. They said they had been pinching each other to see who could stand the most pain. There are no demerits in our school; if there were, every girl would be removed at once. We are expected to create reserves of memory. The girls must remember their teachers as they remembered hot chocolate and after-skiing, all in the same warm fog. I disguised the bruises with iodine, and said that girls sometimes slipped and fell during my outdoor classes and sometimes scratched their arms. "*Merci, Mademoiselle,*" said the two sillies. They could have said "*Fräulein*" and been both accurate and understood, but they are also here because of the French. Their parents certainly speak English, because it was needed a few years ago in Frankfurt, but the children may not remember. They are ignorant and new. Everything they see and touch at home is new. Home is built on the top layer of Ur. It is no good excavating; the fragments would be without meaning. Everything within the walls was inlaid or woven or cast or put together fifteen years ago at the very earliest. Every house is like the house of newly wed couples who have been disinherited or say they scorn their families' taste. It is easy to put an X over half your life (I am thinking about the parents now) when you have nothing out of the past before your eyes; when the egg spoon is plastic and the coffee cup newly fired porcelain; when the books have been lost and the silver, if salvaged, sold a long time ago. There are no dregs, except perhaps a carefully sorted collection of snapshots. You have survived and the food you eat is new – even that. There are bananas and avocado pears and plenty of butter. Not even an unpleasant taste in the mouth will remind you.

I have light hair, without a trace of grey, and hazel eyes. I am not fat, because, unlike my colleagues, I do not hide pastry and *petits fours* in my room to eat before breakfast. My calves, I think, are overdeveloped from years of walking and climbing in low-heeled shoes. I am a bit sensitive about it, and wear my tweed skirts longer than the fashion. Because I take my gloves off in all weather, my hands are rough; their untended appearance makes the French and Italian parents think I am not gently bred. I use the scents and creams my pupils present me with at Christmas. I have few likes and dislikes, but have lost the habit of eating whatever is put before me. I do not mind accepting gifts.

Everyone's father where I come from was a physician or a professor. You will never hear of a father who rinsed beer glasses in a hotel for his keep, or called at houses with a bottle of shampoo and a portable hair-drying machine. Such fathers may have existed, but we do not know about them. My father was a professor of Medieval German. He was an amateur botanist and taught me the names of flowers before I could write. He went from Munich to the university at Debrecen, in the Protestant part of Hungary, when I was nine. He did not care for contemporary history and took no notice of passing events. His objection to Munich was to its prevailing church, and the amount of noise in the streets. The year was 1937. In Debrecen, on a Protestant islet, he was higher and stonier and more Lutheran than anyone else, or thought so. Among the very few relics I have is *Wild Flowers of Germany: One Hundred Pictures Taken from Nature*. The cover shows a spray of Solomon's-seal – five white bells on a curving stem. It seems to have been taken against the night. Under each of the hundred pictures is the place and time we identified the flower. The plants are common, but I was allowed to think them rare. Beneath a photograph of lady's-slipper my father wrote, "By the large wood on the road going towards the vineyard at Durlach July 11 1936," in the same amount of space I needed to record, under snowdrops, "In the Black Forest last Sunday."

I have often wondered whether tears should rise as I leaf through the book; but no – it has nothing to do with me, or with anyone now. It would be a poor gesture to throw it away, an act of harshness or impiety, but if it were lost or stolen I would not complain.

I recall, in calm woods, my eyes on the ground, searching for poisonous mushrooms. He knocked them out of the soft ground with his walking stick, and I conscientiously trod them to pulp. I teach my pupils to do the same, explaining that they may in this way save countless lives; but while I am still talking the girls have wandered away along the sandy paths, chattering, collecting acorns. "Beware of mushrooms that grow around birch trees," I warn. It is part of the lesson.

I can teach in Hungarian, German, French, English, or Italian. I am grateful to Switzerland, where language is a matter of locality, not an imposition, and existence a question of choice. It is better to avoid dying unless the circumstances are clear. If I fall, by accident, out of the funicular tomorrow, it will only prove once again that the suicide rate is high in a peaceful society. In any case, I will see the shadow of the cable car sliding over trees. In a clearing, a woman sorting apples for cider will not look up, although her children may wave. There I shall be, gazing down in order to frighten my vertigo away (I have been trying this for years), in the cable car of my own will, hoping I shall not open the door without meaning to and fall out and become a reproach to a country that has been more than kind. Imagine gliding – floating down to them! Think of the silence, the turning trees! Sometimes I have thought of adopting a strict religion and living by codes and signs, but as I observe my pupils at their absent-minded rites I find they are all too lax and uncertain. These spoiled girls do not care whether they eat roast veal or fish in parsley sauce on

Fridays – it is all the same monotonous meal. Some say they have never been sure what they may eat Fridays, where the limits are. My father was a non-believer, and my mother followed, but without conviction. He led her into the desert. She died of tuberculosis, not daring to speak of God for fear of displeasing her husband. He never carried a house key, because he wanted his wife to answer the door whatever the hour; that is what he was like. My only living relation now is my mother's sister, who has disinherited me because I remind her of my father. She fetched me to Paris to tell me so – that old, fussy, artificial creature in a flat stuffed with showy trifles. "Proust's maternal grandfather lived on this street," she said severely. What of it? What am I supposed to make of that? She gave me a stiff dark photograph of my mother at her confirmation. My mother clasps her Bible to her breast and stares as if the camera were a house on fire.

What I wanted to comment on was children – children in Switzerland. I rent a large room in a chalet seven minutes from my school. Downstairs is the boisterous Canadian who married her ski instructor when she was a pupil here eleven years ago. She has a loud laugh and veined cheeks. He had to resign his post, and now works in the place near the sawmill where they make hand-carved picture frames. The house is full of animals. On rainy days their dining room smells of old clothes and boiled liver. When I am invited to tea (in mugs, without saucers) and sit in one of the armchairs covered with shredded chintz and scraps of blanket, I am obliged to borrow the vacuum cleaner later so as to get the animal hairs out of my skirt. One room is kept free for lodgers – skiers in winter, tourists in summer. In August there were five people in the room – a family of middle-aged parents, two boys, and a baby girl. Because of the rain the boys were restless and the baby screamed with anger and frustration. I took them all to the woods to gather mushrooms.

"If a mushroom has been eaten by a snail, that means it is not poisonous," said the father. Rain dripped through the pine trees. We wore boots and heavy coats. The mother was carrying the bad-tempered baby and could not bend down and search, but now and then she would call, "Here's one that must be safe, because it has been nibbled."

"How do you know the snail is not lying dead somewhere?" I asked.

"You must not make the boys lose confidence in their father," the mother said, trying to laugh, but really a little worried.

"Even if it kills them?" I wanted to say, but it would have spoiled the outing.

My mother said once, "You can tell when mushrooms are safe, because when you stir them the spoon won't tarnish. Poisonous mushrooms turn the spoon black."

"How do you know everyone has a silver spoon?" said my father. He looked at her seriously, with his light eyes. They were like the eyes of birds when he was putting a question. He was not trying to catch her out; he was simply putting the question. That was what I was trying to do. You can warn until your voice is extinguished, and still these people will pick anything and take it home and put their fingers in their mouths.

   In Switzerland parents visit their children sometimes, but are always trying to get away. I would say that all parents of all children here are trying to get away. The baby girl, the screamer, was left for most of a day. The child of aging parents, she had their worried look, as if brooding on the lessons of the past. She was twenty-six months old. My landlady, who offered to keep her amused so that the parents and the two boys could go off on their own for once, had cause to regret it. They tricked the baby cruelly, taking her out to feed melon rinds to Coco, the donkey, in his enclosure at the bottom of the garden. When she came back, clutching the empty basket, her family had disappeared. The baby said something that sounded like "Mama-come-auto" and, writhing like a fish when she was held, slipped away and crawled up the stairs. She called upstairs and down, and the former ski instructor and his wife cried, "Yes, that's it! Mama-come-auto!" She reached overhead to door handles, but the rooms were empty. At noon they tried to make her eat the disgusting purée of carrots and potatoes the mother had left behind. "What if we spanked her?" said the former ski instructor, wiping purée from his sleeve. "Who, you?" shouted his wife. "You wouldn't have nerve enough to brain a mad dog." That shows how tough they thought the baby was. Sometimes during that year-long day, she forgot and let us distract her. We let her turn out our desks and pull our letters to bits. Then she would remember suddenly and look about her with elderly despair, and implore our help, in words no one understood. The weeping grew less frightened and more broken-hearted towards the end of the afternoon. It must have been plain to her then that they would never return. Downstairs they told each other that if she had not been lied to and deceived, then the mother would never have had a day's rest; she had been shut up in the rain in a chalet with this absolute tyrant of a child. The tyrant lay sleeping on the floor. The house was still except for her shuddering breath. Waking, she spoke unintelligible words. They had decided downstairs to pretend not to know; that is, they would not say "Yes, Mama-come-auto" or anything else. We must all three behave as if she had been living here forever and had never known anyone but us. How much memory can be stored in a mind that has not even been developed? What she understood was that we were too deaf to hear her cries and too blind to see her distress. She took the hand of the former ski instructor and dragged it to her face so that he could feel her tears. She was still and slightly feverish when the guilty parents and uneasy boys returned. Her curls were wet through and lay flat on her head. "She was perfect," the landlady said. "Just one little burst of tears after you left. She ate up all her lunch." The mother smiled and nodded, as if giving thanks. "Children are always better away from their parents," she said, with regret. Later, the landlady repeated, to me, as if I had not been there, a strange but believable version of that day, in which the baby cried only once.

That was an exceptional case, where everyone behaved with the best intentions; but what I have wanted to say from the beginning is, do not confide your children to strangers. Watch

the way the stranger holds a child by the wrist instead of by the
hand, even when a hand has been offered. I am thinking
of Véronique, running after the stranger she thought was
making off with the imitation-leather bag that held her cardigan, mustard, salt, pepper, a postcard of the Pont-Neuf, a pink
handkerchief, a peppermint, and a French centime. This was at
the air terminal at Geneva. I thought I might help – interpret
between generations, between the mute and the deaf, so to
speak – but at that moment the woman rushing away with the
bag stopped, shifted it from right hand to left, and grasped
Véronique by the wrist.

I had just been disinherited by my aunt, and was extremely
sensitive to all forms of injustice. I thought that Véronique's
father and mother, because they were not here at the exact
moment she feared her bag was being stolen, had lost all claim
to her, and had I been dispensing justice, would have said so. It
was late in June. My ancient aunt had made me a present of a
Geneva–Paris round-trip tourist-class ticket for the purpose of
telling me to my face why she had cut me out of her will:
I resembled my father, and had somehow disappointed her. I
needed a lesson. She did not say what the lesson would be, but
spoke in the name of Life, saying that Life would teach me. She
was my only relative, that old woman, my mother's eldest sister,
who had had the foresight to marry a French officer in 1919
and spend the next forty years and more saying "Fie." She was
never obliged to choose between duty and self-preservation, or
somehow hope the two would coincide. He was a French
officer and she made his sense of honour hers. He doted on her.
She was one of the lucky women.

Véronique was brought aboard at Orly Airport after everyone else in the Caravelle had settled down. She was led by a pretty stewardess, who seemed bothered by her charge. "Do you mind having her beside you?" she asked. I at first did not see Véronique, who was behind the stewardess, held by the wrist. I placed her where she could look out, and the stewardess disappeared. This would be of more interest if Véronique were now revealed to be a baby ape or a tamed and lovable bear, but she was a child. The journey is a short one – fifty minutes. Some of the small girls in my school arrive alone from Teheran and Mexico City and are none the worse for the adventure. Mishaps occur when they think that pillows or blankets lent them were really presents, but any firm official can deal with that. The child is tossed from home to school, or from one acrobat parent to the other, and knows where it will land. I am frightened when I imagine the bright arc through space, the trusting flight without wings. Reflect on that slow drop from the cable car down the side of the mountain into the trees. The trees will not necessarily catch you like a net.

I fastened her seat belt, and she looked up at me to see what was going to happen next. She had been dressed for the trip in a blue-and-white cotton frock, white socks, and black shoes with a buttoned strap. Her hair was parted in the middle and contained countless shades of light brown, like a handful of autumn grass. There was a slight cast in one eye, but the gaze was steady. The buckle of the seat belt slid down and rested on one knee. She held on to a large bucket bag – held it tightly by its red handle. In the back of the seat before her, along with a map of the region over which we were to fly, were her return

ticket and her luggage tags, and a letter that turned out to be a
letter of instructions. She was to be met by a Mme. Bataille,
who would accompany her to a *colonie de vacances* at Gsteig. I
read the letter towards the end of the trip, when I realized that
the air hostess had forgotten all about Véronique. I am against
prying into children's affairs – even "How do you like your
school?" is more inquisitive than one has a right to be.
However, the important facts about Mme. Bataille and Gsteig
were the only ones Véronique was unable to supply. She talked
about herself and her family, in fits and starts, as if unaware of
the limits of time – less than an hour, after all – and totally
indifferent to the fact that she was unlikely ever to see me
again. The place she had come from was "Orly," her destination was called "the mountains," and the person meeting her
would be either "Béatrice" or "Catherine" or both. That came
later; the first information she sweetly and generously offered
was that she had twice been given injections in her right arm. I
told her my name, profession, and the name of the village
where I taught school. She said she was four but "not yet four
and a half." She had been visiting, in Versailles, her mother and
a baby brother, whose name she affected not to know – an
admirable piece of dignified lying. After a sojourn in the
mountains she would be met at Orly Airport by her father and
taken to the sea. When would that be? "Tomorrow." On the
promise of tomorrow, either he or the mother of the nameless
brother had got her aboard the plane. The Ile-de-France
receded and spread. She sucked her mint sweet, and accepted
mine, wrapped, and was overjoyed when I said she might put it
in her bag, as if a puzzle about the bag had now been solved.

The stewardess snapped our trays into place and gave us identical meals of cold sausage, Russian salad in glue, savory pastry, canned pears, and tinned mineral water. Véronique gazed onto a plateau of food nearly at shoulder level, and picked up a knife and fork the size of gardening tools. "I can cut my meat," she said, meaning to say she could not. The voice that had welcomed us in Paris and had implored Véronique and me to put out our cigarettes now emerged, preceded by crackling sounds, as if the air were full of invisible fissures: "If you look to your right, you will see the city of Dijon." Véronique quite properly took no notice. "I am cold," she stated, knowing that an announcement of one's condition immediately brings on a change for the better. I opened the plastic bag and found a cardigan – hand-knit, light blue, with pearl buttons. I wondered when the change-over would come, when she would have to stop saying "I am cold" in order to grow up without being the kind of person who lets you know that there is a draft in the room, or the beach is too crowded, or the service in the restaurant has gone off. I have pupils who still cannot find their own cardigans, and my old aunt is something of a complainer, as her sister never was. Despite my disinheritance, I was carrying two relics – a compote spoon whose bowl was in the form of a strawberry leaf, and the confirmation photograph of my mother. They weighed heavily in my hand luggage. The weight of the picture was beyond description. I knew that they would be too heavy, yet I held out my hand greedily for more of the past; but my aunt's ration stopped there.

The well-mannered French girl beside me would not drink the water I had poured into her glass until advised she could.

She held the glass in both hands and got it back in its slot without help. Specks of parsley now floated on the water. I said she might leave the remains of the cold sausage, which she was chewing courageously. Giddy with indiscipline, she had some of the salad and all of the pear, and asked, indicating the savory pastry, "Is that something to eat?"

"You can, but it's boring." She had never heard food referred to in that way, and hesitated. As I had left mine, she did not know what the correct attitude ought to be, and after one bite put her spoon down. I think she liked it but, not having understood "boring," was anxious to do the right thing. With her delicate fingers she touched the miniature salt and pepper containers and the doll's tube of mustard, asking what they were for. I remembered that some of the small girls in the school saved them as tokens of travel, and I said, "They are for children to keep."

"Why?"

"I don't know. Some children keep them."

I wondered if this was a mistake, and if she would begin taking things that did not belong to her. She curled her hand around the little mustard tube and said she would keep it for *Maman*. Now that she was wearing the cardigan, her purse was empty save for a mint sweet. I told her that a bag was to put things in, and she said she knew, looking comically worldly. I gave her a centime, a handkerchief, a postcard – searching my own purse to see what could be spared. The stewardess let us descend the ramp from the plane as if she had never seen Véronique before, and no one claimed her. I had great difficulty finding anyone at the terminal who knew anything about Mme. Bataille. When I caught sight of Véronique, later, hurrying desperately after a uniformed woman who did not slow her pace for a second, I feared that *was* Mme. Bataille; but fifteen minutes after that I saw Véronique in the bus that was to take us to the railway station. She was next to a mild, thin, harassed-looking person, who seemed exhausted at the thought of the journey to come.

Now, mark the change in Véronique: She shook out her hair and made it untidy, and stood on the seat and jumped up and down.

"You are a very lucky little girl, going to the mountains *and* the sea," said Mme. Bataille, in something of a whine. Véronique took no more notice of this than she had of Dijon, except to remark that she was going to the seashore tomorrow.

"Not tomorrow. You've only just arrived."

"Tomorrow!" The voice rose and trembled dangerously. "Papa is meeting me at Orly."

"Yes," said the stupid woman soothingly, "but not tomorrow. In August. This is June."

The seats between us were now filled. When I next heard Véronique, the corruption of memory had set in.

"It was the stewardess who cut up your meat," said Mme. Bataille.

"No, a lady."

"A lady in a uniform. The lady you were with when I met you."

"*No.*"

The reason I could hear them was that they were nearly shouting.

Presently, all but giving in, Mme. Bataille said, "Well, she was nice, the lady. I mean, the stewardess."

Two ideas collided: Véronique remembered the woman fairly well, even though the flight no longer existed, but Mme. Bataille knew it was the stewardess.

"I came all alone," said Véronique.

"Who cut your meat, then?"

"I did," said Véronique, and there was no shaking her.

II

Even if Peter Dobay had not instantly recognized me and called my name, my attention would have been drawn by the way he and his wife looked at the station of our village. They got out of the train from Montreux and stood as if dazed. One imagined them blinking behind their sunglasses. At that time of year, we saw only excursion parties – stout women with grey curls, or serious hikers who would stamp from the station through the village and up the slopes. Peter wore a dark suit and black shoes, his wife a black-and-white silk dress, a black silk coat, and fragile open sandals. Her blond hair had been waved that day. I wondered how she would walk in the village streets on her thin high heels.

When we were face to face, Peter and I said together, "What are *you* doing here?"

"I live here – I teach," I said.

"No!" Turning to his wife, he said excitedly, "You know who this is, don't you? It's Erika." Then, back to me, "We've come up to see my wife's twins. They're in a summer school here."

"Better than dragging them round with us," said his wife, in a low-pitched, foggy voice. "They're better off in the fresh air." She touched my arm as if she had always known me and said, "I just can't believe I've finally seen you. Poodlie, it's like a *dream*."

I was faced with two pandas – those glasses! Who was Poodlie? Peter, evidently, yet he called her "Poodlie," too: "Poodlie, it's wonderful," he said, as if she were denying it. His wife? Her voice was twenty years older than his.

He went off to see to their luggage and she stopped seeing me, abruptly, as if now that he was gone nothing was needed. She looked at the village – as much as she could see, which was the central street and the station and the shutters of the station buffet. All I could see was her mouth and the tight pinpoint muscles around it, and the flour dusting of face powder.

"Well?" she said when Peter returned.

"I can't believe it," he said to me, and laughed. "*Here!* What are you doing *here*?"

"I teach," I began again.

"No, here at the station, now, on Sunday."

"Oh, that. I was waiting for the train with the Sunday papers."

"I told you," he cried to his wife. "Remember it was one of the things I said. Even if Erika was starving, she'd buy news-papers. I never knew anyone to read so many papers."

"I haven't had to choose between starving and reading," I said, which was a lie. I watched with regret the bale of papers carted off to the kiosk. In half an hour, those I wanted would be gone.

"*We're* starving," he said. "You'll have lunch with us, won't you? Now?"

"It's early," I said, glancing at his wife.

"Call it breakfast, then." He began guiding us both towards the buffet, his arms around our shoulders in a peasant-like bonhomie that was not like anything I remembered of him.

"The luggage, Poodlie," said his wife.

"He'll take it to the hotel."

"What hotel?"

"The biggest."

"Then it's there," I said, and pointed to an Alpine fortified castle, circa 1912, of yellowish stone, propped behind the street as if on a ledge.

"Good," he said. "Now our lunch."

That was how, on a cool bright day, just before the start of term, I saw Peter again.

In the dark buffet, Peter and his wife kept their glasses on. It seemed part of their personal decorum. Although the clock had only just struck twelve, the restaurant was nearly filled, and we were given a table between the serving pantry and the door. I understood that this was Peter, even though he didn't look at all like the man I had known, and that I was sharing his table. I avoided looking at him. Across the room, over an ocean of heads, was an open window, geraniums, the mountains, and the sky.

"You have beautiful eyes," said Peter's wife. Her voice, like a ventriloquist's, seemed to come from the wrong place – from behind her sunglasses. "Poodlie never told me that. They look like topazes or something like that."

"Yes," said Peter. "Semiprecious stones from the snow-capped mountains of South America."

He sounded like a pompous old man. His English was smooth as cream now, and better than mine. I spoke it with too many people who had accents. Answering a question of his wife's, I heard myself making something thick and endless out of the letter "t": "It is crowded because it is Sunday. Tourists come for miles around. The food in the buffet is celebrated."

"We'll see," said Peter, and took the long plastic-covered menu with rather an air.

His wife was attentive to me. Parents of pupils always try to make me eat more than I care to, perhaps thinking that I would be less intractable if I were less thin. "Your daughter is not only a genius but will make a brilliant marriage," I am supposed to say over caramel cake. I let myself be coaxed by Peter's wife into having a speciality of the place – something monstrous, with boiled meat and dumplings that swam in broth. Having arranged this, she settled down to her tea and toast. As for Peter – well, what a performance! First he read the whole menu aloud and grimaced at everything; then he asked for a raw onion and a bunch of radishes and two pots of yoghurt, and cut up the onions and radishes in the yoghurt

and ate the whole mess with a spoon. It was like the frantic
exhibition of a child who has been made uneasy.

"He isn't well," said his wife, quite as though he weren't
there. "He treats it like a joke, but you know, he was in jail
after the Budapest uprising, and he was so badly treated that it
ruined his stomach. He'll never be the same again."

He did not look up or kick me under the table or in any
manner ask me not to betray him. It occurred to me he had
forgotten I knew. I felt my face flushing, as if I had been boiled
in the same water as the beef and dumplings. I thought I would
choke. I looked, this time with real longing, at the mountain
peaks. They seem so near in the clear weather that sometimes
innocent foot travellers set off thinking they will be there in
three-quarters of an hour. The pockets of snow looked as if
they could have been scooped up with a coffee spoon. The
cows on the lower slopes were the size of thimbles.

"Do you ski at this time of year?" said Peter's wife, without
turning to see what I was staring at.

"One can, but I don't go up any more. There's an hour-
and-a-half walk to the middle station, and the road isn't
pleasant. It's all slush and mud." I thought they would ask
what "the middle station" meant, but they didn't, which
meant they weren't really listening.

When I refused a pudding, Peter said, with his old teasing,
"I told you she was frugal. Her father was a German professor
at Debrecen, the Protestant university."

"So was yours," said his wife sharply, as though reminding
him of a truth he forgot from time to time.

"It never affected me," said Peter, smiling.

"That's where you met, then," said his wife, taking her eyes from me at last.

"No," said Peter. "We were only children then. We met when we were grown up, at the University of Lausanne. It was a coincidence, like meeting today. Erika and I will probably meet – I don't know where. On the moon."

It is difficult enough to listen to someone lying without looking shocked, but imagine what it might be to be part of the fantasy; his lies were a whirlwind, and I was at the core, trying to recognize something familiar. We met in Lausanne; that was true. We met on a bench in the public gardens. I told him I had lived in Hungary and could speak a few sentences of Hungarian still. He was four years younger than I. I told him about my father in Debrecen, and that we were Germans, and that my father had been shot by a Russian soldier. I said I was grateful for Switzerland. He told me he was a half Jew from Budapest and had been ill-used. His life had been saved in some remarkable way by a neutral embassy. He was grateful, too.

He was the first person to whom I had ever spoken spontaneously and without reserve. We met every day for ten days, and when he wanted to leave Switzerland because he thought it would be better somewhere else and would not go without me, I did not think twice. The evening lamps went on in the park where we were sitting, and I thought that if I did not go with him I would suffer every evening for the rest of my life, every time the lamps were lit. To avoid suffering, I went with him. Yet when I told my father's old friends, the people who had taken me in and welcomed me and kept me from starving, I said it was my duty. I said it was Peter who could not live without me. It is true I would never have gone out of Switzerland, out to the wilderness, but for him. My father had friends at the University of Lausanne, and although after the war some were afraid, because the wind had shifted, others took me in when I was seventeen and homeless and looked after me until I could work. I was afraid of telling about Peter. In the end, I had to. I quoted something my father had once said about duty, and no one could contradict that.

It lasted only a short time, the adventure, and can be briefly and accurately remembered. Quickly, then: He had heard there was a special university for refugees in a city on the Rhine, and thought they might admit him. We lived in a hotel over a café, and discovered we were living in a brothel. The university existed, but its quota was full. We were starving to death. We were so attractive a couple, so sympathetic-looking, that people dulled with eating looked at us fondly. We strolled along the Rhine and looked at excursion boats. "Your duty is always before you, plain as that," my father had said, pointing with his walking stick to some vista or tree or cloud. I do not know what he was pointing at – something in his mind.

Because of Peter I was on a sea without hope of landing anywhere. It grew on me that he had been jealous of my safety and had dragged me beyond my depth. There had been floods – I think in Holland – and money was being collected for the victims. Newspapers spoke of "Rhine solidarity," and I was envious, for I had solidarity with no one now. It took me time to think things out, for I had no illusions about my intelligence, and I wondered finally why I did not feel any solidarity with Peter. I loved him, but together we would starve or drown.

"You can't stay here," said the owner of the hotel one day. "It isn't safe for refugees. We have the police in too often."

"We can't move," said Peter. "My wife is ill." But that did not give me a feeling of solidarity, for I was not his wife, and he was a person who would keep moving from one place to another.

He never told the same story twice, except for some details. He said he was picked up and deported when he was ten or twelve. He was able to describe the Swiss or Swedish consulate where they tried to save him. In his memories, the person who hid him was always different. Sometimes he said it was a peasant, sometimes a fat woman who shut him in a cupboard. The forced march must have been true. Someone – he did not say who – was working on his behalf. He hinted he was illegitimate, and that a person of noble birth, who did not wish to be known, was his protector. It is true that sometimes in the marches from Budapest to the border one person in the column was saved, if the order came through in time. It was often at night. The column stopped by the side of the road, and the torches, hooded because of the air raids, moved from face to face. One night, the light picked out an old man who would have died soon in any case, and Peter. He could not see his deliverers – he saw the light moving from face to face. The light was lowered. He tried to hide, but they spoke his name. He thought the light meant an execution. He was taken away in a car, back to Budapest, and in the car was comforted with chocolates. These were the details he repeated: the light on his face, the voice saying his name, and the chocolates. Sometimes, being boastful, he said he was active in the Arrow Cross Party; but he was a victim, and a child. Once, he said he was poor and had sold papers in the street to pay for his shoes. But he was such a liar. He may have been poor, or he may have been from a solid family who lost him along the way; but it was not a Protestant family, and his father was not a professor at Debrecen. Also, he was not in Budapest during the uprising in 1956. He was in a city on the Rhine, starving, with me.

We stood at the foot of the cathedral in this city one day. We had nothing to eat and nothing to do. I could not understand why Peter had brought me here or what he wanted now. He urged me to write my father's old friends in Lausanne, or to my aunt in Paris, but I was proud, and ashamed that he would ask such a thing. I think he believed I was a magic solution just in myself. He lived in a fantasy of false names, false fortunes, false parents, and here was a reality of expired visas and dry bread he could not explain away.

"Goethe climbed to the top of this cathedral to cure himself of vertigo. You should try it," Peter said.

"Oh, Goethe would," I said, and that was the only thing that autumn that made Peter laugh. We climbed and climbed, and looked down at matchbox cars. I felt vertigo, and was surprised he did not. I held out my arms to receive him if he fainted – I was so sure he would not stand this – but he stood smiling down with no intention of toppling over. Below was the sweet nursery world, nursery-sized, with toy trains and toy people. It smiled back at him; he was its lord, at least from up here. My world was my size, and often bigger. I was afraid of the shrunken world as he saw it; he made me unsteady. I left him that day. He went alone to the post office to see if there were phantom letters from ghost friends, and I made myself as tidy as I could and went to my own consulate with a plausible story. And that was the last Peter saw of me, until Peter, or Poodlie, called my name at the station.

I don't know what he remembered. He had taken my family as his, and expected me to smile. Actually, I did. I made him a present of my family. But by now he must have believed that whatever came into his head was true, for he did not thank me – neither then nor later. I leaned over the table and said, "I see what is making the difference. It is the dark glasses." He immediately took them off, but I saw that I still did not recognize him.

An excursion party now trooped into the buffet. Their accents were, I think, industrial England over, I think, Viennese. One of the women smeared thick white cream on her sun-burned arms. "Let's finish and pay and get out of here," said Peter's wife, sharply. I stared at him then, but his face showed nothing. He did not add or contribute. It might have had nothing to do with him. She slipped him folded money so that he could pay the bill. I tried to think, but they had stuffed me with food. I clung to one idea: no one would get me out of Switzerland again, as he once had to a city on the Rhine, as my old aunt had got me to Paris. Each time I returned I was wounded, or had failed. Outside the station, I stopped at the kiosk, but of course my newspapers were gone.

The next afternoon, I sat in the lobby of their hotel. His wife now looked through the windows to the station, as if afraid of missing the train out. She poured tea from a leaky pot, and passed chocolate biscuits, shell-shaped, in a thin coating of sugar. They were Poodlie's favourites; she was sorry he wasn't here. She poured with a tense, strong hand – I admired the long fingers, and the short nails, on which the red was thickly spread. Absently but politely, she asked about my work, as if she were a headmistress interviewing me for a post.

I described flowers next to snow, and plants so perfect and minute, rooted on stone, that they must be like the algae on Mars.

"Oh, yes, edelweiss," she said.

He was a parcel posted without an address, and he had come to her. Now I heard her inviting me to join them. I heard the words "The twins would adore you, and he is a different person when you're there. I've never seen him so gay and happy as he was yesterday at lunch." He had put her up to it, and now he was out, walking around in the village, waiting for the barter to be completed. "He has talked about you such a lot," she said.

"What did he tell you?"

"Why, that you were a wonderful person. He said you had been so kind to him."

That part of it ended there. She explained that Peter was walking, not in the village, as I had supposed, but somewhere up a mountain. He had gone up in a cable car. "I didn't bring the right clothes," she said. "We could drive somewhere, but we never do." It was the only sign of her discontent. The person she had gone to consult when she contemplated this marriage – a rapid psychotherapy, she explained – had warned her not to take over too many head-of-the-family functions from a young husband. That meant, among other things, that she was never to drive the car. But Poodlie was too wild to drive. She gave him cars, but could not trust him to drive them. I thought of him wandering along a steep, windy slope now, not knowing how to keep a foothold in his slippery shoes. He was up above the village in his dark suit and dark glasses and shoes. How could she let him go that way – as if he were lost or had strayed from the towns? He was alone, shivering (no one had told him how cold it would be), dreaming and inventing things to be remembered.

I did not meet her children, but I saw her with them in a tearoom: two plump girls of about fourteen, in clay-coloured tights and long pullovers that covered their sturdy hips. They were not girls I had ever seen before. They looked sullen there in the dark shop, which was suffocating with the smell of chocolate. They were choosing éclairs, pointing, discontented and curt. Their school had not yet taught them manners, and their mother, with a stiff smile on her lips and her sunglasses hiding her opinion, could see only the distance between what they were and what they ought to be. She was not an educator. The girls' clumsiness was a twist of the spirit, a sprain. She watched them choose and eat, and I thought how much time she spent watching people choose and eat their food. She removed the glasses and rubbed the space between her eyes. She saw me, and her glance meeting mine almost begged something. Information? Advice? She had the psychotherapy for advice, and she had Peter to tell her stories. Perhaps she wanted me to change my mind about going with them. He must have asked for me, as he asked for cars she would not let him drive because he broke them.

It would have been easy for her to make me believe my choices were wrong, but it would have been another matter to make me change my mind. Once when she was busy with the twins, he came to me. He looked at the saucer full of moss and Alpine plants; and the shelf with tea and hard biscuits and cereal and powdered milk; and at my bed with its shabby cushions; and my walls decorated with photographs of snow and skiers – searching for something. He twitched a curtain as if it hid a view he liked and said, "It's all dirty green, like a customs inspector's uniform."

But I had travelled nearly as much as Peter, and over some of the same frontiers. He could not impress me. I think (like the remark about semiprecious stones and snow-capped mountains) it was a way of talking he had developed because it amused his wife. He knew it was no good talking about the past, because we were certain to remember it differently. He daren't be nostalgic about anything, because of his inventions. He would never be certain if the memory he was feeling tender about was true.

I watched him at the window – the town lad, hating the quiet. "What is that racket?" he said angrily. It was the stream running outside through the garden. There was also Coco, the donkey, braying in his enclosure. He would have preferred a deafening, continued, city noise. I remembered him on streets full of trains and traffic; I remembered the quick turn of his head. When I remembered the horror of the room over the café, I thought it had been the horror of living on a street.

The view here, after the long garden, was of the roof of the chalet farther down the slope. A crash: my bookshelf, containing

Wild Flowers of Germany, fell from the wall. The house shook.

He looked at the perpendicular, windless rain that had begun to fall. He turned back to the room; he was still searching. "You used to read," he said, still in pursuit of something. I pointed to the floor. "Didn't you hear them fall?" He made a silly remark – I remember the sense of it, not the words. He could not trust me, because I had once run away, vanished, but as he had long ago fabricated something else, he could not remember why he could not trust me. The room grew dark. I served coffee in cups with *Liberté* and *Patrie* and a green-and-white shield of the Vaud on them. The parents of a pupil had bought them in Montreux for me once. He held his cup close to his eyes and read the words, and put it down without saying anything.

I said to myself that he was only a man about whom I had known a great deal and it was so long ago that much of it might have been told to me by someone else. Nostalgia is a weakness; he would be the one to indulge in it, if he dared. I had not gone to him out of duty and had not left him out of self-preservation. It was not that simple. I would have talked, for I knew he was waiting for me to scrape away the dreams and begin again with the truth, but I thought, I shall write him a letter. That will be easier. I shall write about everything, all of the truth.

They came up by train and they left by train – the little red train that has its start among the hotels and swimming pools along the lake. As neither of them could drive the other, they had to take the train. They were leaving the twins behind. The twins were happy, and the fresh air was doing them good. They were enrolled for the autumn term.

The first-class carriages of those trains look as if they had been built for miniature royal tours. There are oval satinwood panels and Art Nouveau iron roses. Some of the roses had iron worms eating their hearts. I imagine the artist meant something beautiful and did not know it was hideous. As you can imagine, the trains are beautifully polished. The panels gleam, and dust is not allowed to accumulate in the rose petals. The windows are clear for a view of cows and valleys, the ashtrays are emptied and polished, and the floors are swept. I like best the deep-rose velvet, with its pattern of brown leaves and ferns, that covers the seats. It wears slowly; in some very worn places the colour is light apricot and the palest lemon, and the pattern can scarcely be seen. Somewhere in storage, preserved from dust and the weather, are bales of the same velvet, and when a seat becomes too worn they simply patch it up again.

He would have stayed if I had wanted. Yes, Poodlie would have left Poodlie. He knew *I* would never go with them. I might have been for sale, but not to her. At a word of truth he would have stayed, if only to hear the rest. He would have made furious plans, and left such an imprint on this place that after his departure I could not have lived here any more. Or perhaps this time one of us would have stayed forever. These are the indecisions that rot the fabric, if you let them. The shutter slams to in the wind and sways back; the rain begins to slant as the wind increases. This is the season for mountain storms. The wind rises, the season turns; no autumn is quite like another. The autumn children pour out of the train, and the clouds descend the mountain slopes, and there we are with walls and a ceiling to the village. Here is the pattern on the carpet where he walked, and the cup he drank from. I have learned to be provident. I do not waste a sheet of writing paper, or a postage stamp, or a tear. The stream outside the window, deep with rain, receives rolled in a pellet the letter to Peter. Actually, it is a blank sheet on which I intended to write a long letter about everything – about Véronique. I have wasted the sheet of paper. There has been such a waste of everything; such a waste.

Ernst in Civilian Clothes

———————————■———————————

Opening a window in Willi's room to clear the room of cigarette smoke, Ernst observes that the afternoon sky has not
changed since he last glanced at it a day or two ago. It is a thick
winter blanket, white and grey. Nothing moves. The black
cobbles down in the courtyard give up a design of wet light.
More light behind the windows now, and the curtains become
glassy and clear. The life behind them is implicit in its privacy.
Forms are poised at stove and table, before mirrors, insolently
unconcerned with Ernst. His neighbours on this court in the
rue de Lille in Paris do not care if he peers at them, and he, in
turn, may never be openly watched. Nevertheless, he never

switches on the table lamp, dim though it is, without fastening Willi's cretonne curtains together with a safety pin. He feels so conspicuous in his new civilian clothes, idling the whole day, that it would not astonish him if some civic-minded and diligent informer had already been in touch with the police.

On a January afternoon, Ernst the civilian wears a nylon shirt, a suede tie, a blazer with plastic buttons, and cuffless trousers so tapered and short that when he sits down they slide to his calf. His brown military boots – unsuccessfully camouflaged for civilian life with black Kiwi – make him seem anchored. These are French clothes, and, all but the boots, look as if they had been run up quickly and economically by a little girl. Willi, who borrowed the clothes for Ernst, was unable to find shoes his size, but is pleased, on the whole, with the results of his scrounging. It is understood (by Willi) that when Ernst is back in Germany and earning money, he will either pay for the shirt, tie, blazer, and trousers or else return them by parcel post. Ernst will do neither. He has already forgotten the clothes were borrowed in Willi's name. He will forget he lived in Willi's room. If he does remember, if a climate one day brings back a January in Paris, he will simply weep. His debts and obligations dissolve in his tears. Ernst's warm tears, his good health, and his poor memory are what keep him afloat.

In an inside pocket of the borrowed jacket are the papers that show he is not a deserter. His separation from the Foreign Legion is legal. For reasons not plain this afternoon, his life is an endless leave without the hope and the dread of return to the barracks. He is now like any man who has begged for a

divorce and was shocked when it was granted. The document
has it that he is Ernst Zimmermann, born in 1927, in Mainz. If
he were to lose that paper, he would not expect any normal
policeman to accept his word of honour. He is not likely to
forget his own name, but he could, if cornered, forget the connection between an uncertified name and himself. Fortunately,
his identification is given substance by a round purple stamp
on which one can read *Préfecture de Police*. Clipped to the certificate is a second-class railway ticket to Stuttgart, where
useful Willi has a brother-in-law in the building trade. Willi
has written that Ernst is out of the Legion, and needs a job,
and is not a deserter. The brother-in-law is rich enough to be
jovial; he answers that even if Ernst is a deserter he will take
him on. This letter perplexes Ernst. What use are papers if the
first person you deal with as a civilian does not ask to see even
copies of them? What is Ernst, if his papers mean nothing? He
knows his name and his category (ex-Legionnaire) but not
much more. He does not know if he is German or Austrian.
His mother was Austrian and his stepfather was German. He
was born before Austria became Germany, but when he was
taken prisoner by the Americans in April, 1945, Austria and
Germany were one. Austrians are not allowed to join the
Foreign Legion. If he were Austrian now and tried to live
in Austria, he might be in serious trouble. Was he German or
Austrian in September, 1945, when he became a Legionnaire
because the food was better on their side of the prison camp?
His mother *is* Austrian, but he has chosen the stepfather; he is
German. He looks at the railway posters with which Willi has

decorated the room, and in a resolution that must bear a date (January 28, 1963) he decides, My Country. A new patriotism, drained from the Legion, flows over a field of daffodils, the casino at Baden-Baden, a gingerbread house, part of the harbor at Hamburg, and a couple of sea gulls.

Actually, there may be misstatements in his papers. Only his mother, if she is still living, and still cares, could make the essential corrections. He was really born in the Voralberg in 1929. When he joined the Legion, he said he was eighteen, for there were advantages in both error and accuracy then; prisoners under eighteen received double food rations, but prisoners who joined the Foreign Legion thought it was the fastest way home. Ernst is either thirty-four or thirty-six. He pledged his loyalty to official papers years ago – to officers, to the Legion, to stamped and formally attested facts. It is an attested fact that he was born in Mainz. Mainz is a place he passed through once, in a locked freight car, when he was being transported to France with a convoy of prisoners. He does not know why the Americans who took him prisoner in Germany sent him to France. Willi says to this day that the Americans sold their prisoners at one thousand five hundred francs a head, but Ernst finds such suppositions taxing. During one of the long, inexplicable halts on the mysterious voyage, where arrival and travelling were equally dreaded, another lad in man's uniform, standing crushed against Ernst, said, "We're in Mainz." "Well?" "Mainz is finished. There's nothing left." "How do you know? We can't see out," said Ernst. "There is nothing left anywhere for us," said the boy. "My father says this is the Apocalypse."

What an idiot, Ernst felt; but later on, when he was asked where he came from, he said, without hesitating, and without remembering why, "Mainz."

Ernst is leaving Paris tomorrow morning. He will take the Métro to the Gare de l'Est at an hour when the café windows are fogged with the steam of rinsed floors. The Métro quais will smell of disinfectant and cigarette butts. Willi will probably carry his duffelbag and provide him with bread and chocolate to eat on the train. He is leaving before he is deported. He has no domicile and no profession; he is a vagabond without a home (his home was the Legion) and without a trade (his trade was the Legion, too). Some ex-Legionnaires have come out of it well. András is a masseur, Thomas a car washer, Carlo lives with a prostitute, Dietrich is a night watchman, Vieko has a scholarship and is attending courses in French civilization, Piotr is seen with a smart interior decorator, Lothar is engaged to marry a serious French girl. Ernst has nothing, not even his pension. He waited for the pension, but now he has given up. He is not bitter but feels ill-used. Also, he thinks he looks peculiar. He has not been to Germany since he was carried through Mainz eighteen years ago, and he is wearing civilian clothes as normal dress for the first time since he was seven years old.

His Austrian mother was desperately poor even after she married his stepfather, and when Ernst put on his Hitler Youth uniform at seven, it meant, mostly, a great saving in clothes. He has been in uniform ever since. His uniforms have not been lucky. He has always been part of a defeated army. He has fought for Germany and for France and, according to what he has been told each time, for civilization.

He wore civilian clothes for one day, years ago, when he was confirmed, and then again when he was sixteen and a Werewolf, but those were not normal occasions. When he was confirmed a Christian, and created a Werewolf, he felt disguised and curiously concealed. He is disguised and foreign to himself today, looking out of Willi's window at the sky and the cobbles and the neighbours in the court. He looks shabby and unemployed, like the pictures of men in German street crowds before the Hitler time.

It is quite dark when the little boy, holding his mother's hand with one hand and a cone with roasted chestnuts in the other, enters the court. The mother pushes the heavy doors that hide the court from the street, and the pair enter slowly, as if they had tramped a long way in heavy snow. They have returned safely, once again, from their afternoon stroll in the Jardin des Tuileries. The chestnuts were bought from the old Algerian beside the pond near the Place de la Concorde. The smoke of the blue charcoal fire was darker than the sky, and the smell of chestnuts burning is more pungent than their taste. In a cone of newspaper (a quarter-page of *France-Soir*) they warm the heart and hand.

Four days ago Ernst followed these two. They live up above Willi's room. He was curious to know where they were going. The walk came to nothing. When the boy and his mother reached the object of their outing – the old man, the chestnuts, the frozen pond – they turned around and came

away, between the black, stripped trees and the cold statues
Ernst thinks of as trees. Mercury is a tree; the Rape of Deidamia
is another tree. They skirted a sea of feeding pigeons, out of
which rose a brave old maniac of a woman with a cotton scarf
on her head. It is an illegal act to scatter crumbs for the birds
of Paris, but on this Siberian day the guardians of the peace
are too frozen to act. The mother, the child, and Ernst behind
them, plod on snow like sifted sugar, past the Roman emper-
ors, past the straw-covered beds of earth. In great peril they
cross the Quai des Tuileries. The traffic light changes from
green to red without warning when they are half over, and
they stand still, creating a whirlpool. Along the Pont Royal
the wind strikes like an enemy, from every direction at once.
After a sunless day there is a pale orange cloud on the Gare
d'Orsay. The spires of Notre-Dame and the stalled buses in
the traffic block on the Pont du Carousel appear nacreous and
white, as if in moonlight. The mother and child are engulfed
and nearly trampled suddenly by released civil servants
running away from their offices behind the Gare d'Orsay.
They run as if there were lions behind them. It has never been
as cold as this in Paris. Breath is visible; Ernst's emerges
from marble lungs. The mother and child face the last hazard
of the journey – the Quai Anatole France. Even when they
have the green light in their favour, they are caught by cars
turning right off the Pont Royal. There are two policemen
here to protect them, and there are traffic lights to be obeyed,
but every person and every thing is submerged by the dark
and the cold and the torrent of motorcars and a fear like a
fear of lions.

Tiring of this, Ernst threads his way across, against the light, leaving the child and the woman trembling on the curb. He had wondered about them, and wondered where they went every day, and now he knows. That was four days ago. He has seldom been out of Willi's room since.

"Hurry," says the mother when she and the child reach the middle of the court. She takes the chestnuts and the boy's gloves, and the child vanishes behind the rotting wooden door of the courtyard lavatory. The mother, waiting, looks up at a window for a friend. She has a crony – a hag Ernst sees in the store where he and she, without speaking, buy the same ink-thick, unlabelled red wine. She buys one litre at a time, Ernst several. Her window is just below his, to the left.

The mother might be twenty-six. She stands in cold light from an open window. Her upturned face is broad and white, the angora beret on her head is white moss. She has wrapped a tatty fur around her neck, like an old Russian countess. Her handbag seems the old displaced-person sort, too – big, and bulging with cancelled passports. She speaks in the thin voice of this city, the high plucked wire of a voice that belittles the universe.

"I've had enough, and I've told him so," she says, without caring who might hear. It sounds at least the start of a tragedy, but then she invites the hag, who, with a tablecloth around her head, is hanging out the window, to stop by and share the television later on. At half past seven there will be a program called *L'Homme du XXe Siècle*.

Ernst followed this woman because she was fit for his attention. He would have sought a meeting somewhere, but the weather was against it. He could not have brought her to Willi's room, because Willi has scruples about gossip and neighbours. Ernst could have gone upstairs (he does not doubt his success for a moment), but the walls are cardboard and he would have drawn notice to his marked civilian self.

Early in the morning, the mother's voice is fresh and quick. The father leaves for work at six o'clock. She takes the child to school at a quarter to eight. The child calls her often: "*Maman*, come here." "*Maman*, look." She rushes about, clattering with brooms. At nine she goes to market, and she returns at ten, calling up to her crony that she has found nothing, nothing fit to eat, but the basket is full of something; she is bent sideways with the weight of it. By noon, after she has gone out once more to fetch the child for lunch, her voice begins to rise. Either the boy refuses what she has cooked for him or does not eat quickly enough, but his meal is dogged with the repeated question "Are you going to obey?" He is dragged back to school weeping. Both are worn out with this, and their late-afternoon walk is exhausted and calm. In the evening the voice climbs still higher. "You will see, when your father comes home!" It is a bird shrieking. Whatever the child has done or said is so monstrously disobedient that she cannot wait for the father to arrive. She has to chase the child and catch him before she can beat him. There is the noise of running, a chair knocked down, something like marbles, perhaps the chestnuts, rolling on the floor. "You *will* obey me!" It is a promise of the future now. The caught child screams. If the house were burning, if there were lions on the stairs, he could not scream more. All round the court the neighbours stay well away from their windows. It is no one's concern. When his mother beats him, the child calls for help, and calls "*Maman*." His true mother will surely arrive and take him away from his mother transformed. Who else can he appeal to? It makes sense. Ernst has heard grown men call for their mothers. He knows about submission and punishment and justice and power. He knows what the child does not know – that the screaming will stop, that everything ends. He did not learn a trade in the Foreign Legion, but he did learn to obey.

Good-natured Willi danced a java this morning, with an imaginary girl in his arms. Fortunately, he had no partner, for she would have been kicked to bits. His thick hands described circles to the music from the radio, and his thick legs kicked sideways and forward. Ernst saw the soles of Willi's shoes and his flying unmilitary hair, and his round face red with laughter. When the music stopped, he stopped, and after he had regained his breath, used it to repeat that he would come home early to cook the stew for their last supper. Willi then went off to work. Today he is guide and interpreter for seventeen men from a German firm that makes bath salts. He will show them the Emperor's tomb and the Eiffel Tower and leave them to their fate up in Pigalle. As Willi neither smokes nor drinks, and is not even objectively interested in pictures of naked dancers, he can see no advantage in spending an evening there. He weighs the free banquet against the waste of time and

chooses time. He will tell them what the limit price is for a
bottle of champagne and abandon them, seventeen of them, in
hats, scarves, overcoats, and well-soled shoes, safe in an estab-
lishment where *Man spricht Deutsch*. Then he will hurry home
to cut up the leeks and carrots for Ernst's last stew. Willi has a
sense of responsibility, and finds most people noisier and sillier
than they were ten years ago. He does not know that ten years
have gone by. His face does not reflect the change of time,
rate, and distance. He is small in stature, as if he had not begun
his adolescent growth. He looks and speaks about as he did
when he and Ernst were prisoners in the west of France eighteen years ago.

This morning, before attending to his seventeen men from
the bath-salts factory, Willi went to the market and came back
with a newspaper someone had dropped in a bus shelter. What
a find! Twenty-five centimes of fresh news! He also had a piece
of stewing beef and a marrow bone, and he unfolded an old
journal to reveal four carrots and two leeks. The grocer
weighed the vegetables and the journal together, so that Willi
was cheated, but he was grateful to be allowed to purchase any
vegetables at all. The only vegetables on public sale that
morning were frozen Brussels sprouts.

"It is like wartime," says Willi, not displeased that it is like
wartime. He might enjoy the privations of another war,
without the killing. He thinks privation is good for people. If
you give Willi a piece of chocolate, he gives half of it away to
someone else and puts the rest aside until it has turned stale
and white. Then he eats it, slowly and thankfully, and says it is
delicious. Lying on the floor, Ernst has watched Willi working

– typing translations at four francs a page. His blunt fingers work rapidly. His eyes never look up from the paper beside the machine. He has taught himself to translate on sight, even subjects about which he cares nothing, such as neon tubes and historical principles. They have come only a short distance from their camp in 1945, where someone said to Ernst, "You have lost the war. You are not ordinary prisoners. You may never go home again." At the other end of the camp, on the far side of a fence, the Foreign Legion recruits played soccer and threw leftover food into garbage cans; and so Ernst left Willi with his bugs, his potato peelings, his diseased feet, his shorn head, and joined the Legion. Willi thought he would get home faster by staying where he was. They were both bad guessers. Willi is still in Paris, typing translations, guiding visiting businessmen, playing S.S. officers in films about the last war. It is a way of living, not quite a life. Ernst teases Willi because he works hard for little money, and because he worries about things of no consequence – why children are spoiled, why girls lose their virtue, why wars are lost, won, or started. He tells Willi, "Do you want to go to your grave with nothing but this behind you?" If Ernst really believes what he says, how can one explain the expression he takes on then, when he suddenly rolls over on the floor and says, "Girls are nothing, Willi. You haven't missed much. You're better off the way you are."

This is a long day without daylight. Ernst's duffelbag is packed. He has nothing to do. He has forgotten that Willi asked him to put the marrow bone and stewing beef in a pan of

water on the electric plate no later than four o'clock. In the
paper found at the bus shelter Ernst discovers that because of
the hard winter – the coldest since 1880 – the poor are to be
given fifty kilos of free coal. Or else it is one hundred and fifty
or one hundred kilos; he cannot understand the news item,
which gives all three figures. Gas is to be free for the poor (if
consumed moderately) until March 31st. Willi's gas heater
flames the whole day, because Ernst, as a civilian, is sensitive to
weather. Ernst will let Willi pay the bill, and, with some iri-
descent memory of something once read, he will believe that
Willi had free gas – and, who knows, perhaps free rent and
light! – all winter long. When Ernst believes an idea suitable
for the moment, it becomes true. He has many troubles, and if
you believe one-tenth of anything he tells you, he will say you
are decent.

Once, Ernst was a Werewolf concealed in civilian clothes.
His uniform was gone, and his arms and identity papers buried
in the mud outside a village whose name he cannot remember.
It begins with "L." He lay on the ground vomiting grass, bark,
and other foods he had eaten. He had been told to get rid of
the papers but not the arms. He disobeyed. He walked all one
night to the town where his mother and stepfather were. The
door was locked, because the forced-labor camps were open
now and ghosts in rags were abroad and people were frightened of them. His mother opened the door a crack when she
recognized the Werewolf's voice (but not his face or his disguise) and she said, "You can't stay here." There was a smell of
burning. They were burning his stepfather's S.S. uniform

in the cellar. Ernst's mother kissed him, but he had already turned away. The missed embrace was a salute to the frightening night, and she shut the door on her son and went back to her husband. Even if she had offered him food, he could not have swallowed. His throat closed on his breath. He could not swallow his own spit. He cannot now remember his own age or what she was like. He is either thirty-four or thirty-six, and born in Mainz.

Willi is always reading about the last war. He cuts up newspapers and pastes clippings in scrapbooks. All this is evidence. Willi is waiting for the lucid, the wide-awake, and above all the rational person who will come out of the past and say with authority, "This was true," and "This was not." The photographs, the films, the documents, the witnesses, and the survivors could have been invented or dreamed. Willi searches the plain blue sky of his childhood and looks for a stain of the evil he has been told was there. He cannot see it. The sky is without spot.

"What was wrong with the Hitler Youth?" says Willi. What was wrong with being told about Goethe Rilke Wagner Schiller Beethoven?

Ernst, when he listens to Willi, seems old and sly. He looks like a corrupted old woman. Many of the expressions of his face are womanish. He is like the old woman who says to the young girl, "Have nothing to do with anyone. Stay as you are." He knows more than Willi because he has been a soldier all his life. He knows that there are no limits to folly and pain except fatigue and the failing of imagination. He has always known

more than Willi, but he can be of no help to him, because of
his own life-saving powers of forgetfulness.

It is the twentieth anniversary of Stalingrad, and the paper
found at the bus stop is full of it. Stalingrad – now renamed –
is so treated that it seems a defeat all around, and a man with a
dull memory, like Ernst, can easily think that France and
Germany fought on the same side twenty years ago. Or else
there were two separate wars, one real and one remembered. It
must have been a winter as cold as this, a winter grey on white
and full of defeat. Ernst turns on the radio and, finding
nothing but solemn music, turns it off. From the court he
hears a romantic tune sung by Charles Aznavour and is moved
by it. On an uncrowded screen a line of ghosts shuffles in
snow, limps through the triumphant city, and a water cart
cleans the pavement their feet have touched. Ernst, the eter-
nally defeated, could know the difference between victory and
failure, if he would apply his mind to it; but he has met young
girls in Paris who think Dien Bien Phu was a French victory,
and he has let them go on thinking it, because it is of no
importance. Ernst was in Indo-China and knows it was a
defeat. There is no fear in the memory. Sometimes another,
younger Ernst is in a place where he must save someone who
calls "*Mutti!*" He advances; he wades in a flooded cellar. There
is more fear in dreams than in life. What about the dream where
someone known – sometimes a man, sometimes a woman –
wears a mask and wig? The horror of the wig! He wakes dry-
throated. Willi has always been ready to die. If the judge he is
waiting for says "This is true, and you were not innocent," he
says he will be ready to die. He could die tomorrow. But Ernst,

who has been in uniform since he was seven, and defeated in every war, has never been prepared.

In the court it snowed and rained and the rain froze on the windows. By three o'clock he could not see without a light. He pinned the curtains together, switched on the table lamp, and lay down on the floor. In the paper he read the following:

A l'occasion d'un premier colloque
européen
LE "DOPING" HUMAIN
a été défini et condamné

It must mean something. Would Willi cut this out and paste it in a scrapbook? Willi, who will be home in two or three hours, is made sick by the smell of cigarette smoke, and so Ernst gets up, undoes the curtains, and airs the room. He must have fallen asleep over the paper, for it is quite dark, and the child and his mother have returned from their walk. The room is cold and smells of the courtyard instead of cigarettes. He shuts the window and curtains and looks for something to read. Willi has saved a magazine article by an eminent author in which it is claimed that young Werewolves were animals. Their training had lowered the barrier between wolves and men. Witnesses heard them howling in the night. When the judge arrives, Willi will say to him, "What about this?" Ernst begins the article but finds it long-winded. He grins, suddenly, reading, without knowing he has shown his teeth. If he were

seen at this moment, an element of folklore would begin to
seep through Europe, where history becomes folklore in a
generation: "On the rue de Lille, a man of either thirty-six or
thirty-four, masquerading in civilian clothes, became a wolf."
He reads: "Witnesses saw them eating babies and tearing live
chickens apart." He buried his arms and his identity in the mud
outside a village whose name he cannot remember. He vomited
bark and grass and the yellow froth of fear. He was in a
peasant's jacket stiff with grease and sweat. Ernst is rusting and
decomposing in the soft earth near a village. Under leaves,
snow, dandelions, twigs, his shame moulders. Without papers he
was no one; without arms he was nothing. Without papers and
without arms he walked as if in a fever, asking himself constantly what he had forgotten. In the village whose name
began with "L," he saw an American. He sat throwing a knife
at a mark on a wall. He would get up slowly, go over to the
wall, pull out the knife, walk slowly back, sit down, balance
the knife, and aim at the mark, holding the knife by the blade.

Ernst is going home, but not to that village. He could never
find it again. He does not know what he will find. Willi, who
goes home every year at Christmas, returns disgusted. He
hates the old men who sit and tell stories. "Old men in their
forties," says Willi, who does not know he will soon be old.
The old men rub their sleeves through beer rings and say that
if the Americans had done this, if von Paulus had done that, if
Hitler had died a year sooner . . . finger through the beer
rings, drawing a line, and an arrow, and a spear.

Having aired the room, and frozen it, Ernst lights another
cigarette. He is going home. In Willi's scrapbook he turns over

unpasted clippings about the terrorist trials in Paris in 1962. Two ex-Legionnaires, deserters, were tried – he will read to the end, if he can keep awake. Two ex-Legionnaires were shot by a firing squad because they had shot someone else. It is a confusing story, because some of the clippings say "bandits" and some say "patriots." He does not quite understand what went on, and the two terrorists could not have understood much, either, because when the death sentence was spoken they took off their French decorations and flung them into the courtroom and cried, "Long Live France!" and "Long Live French Algeria!" They were not French, but they had been in the Legion, and probably did not know there were other things to say. That was 1962 – light-years ago in political time.

Ernst is going home. He has decided, about a field of daffodils, My Country. He will not be shot with "Long Live" anything on his lips. No. He will not put on a new uniform, or continue to claim his pension, or live with a prostitute, or become a night watchman in Paris. What will he do?

When Ernst does not know what to do, he goes to sleep. He sits on the floor near the gas heater with his knees drawn up and his head on his arms. He can sleep in any position, and he goes deeply asleep within seconds. The room is as sealed as a box and his duffelbag an invisible threat in a corner. He wades in the water of a flooded cellar. His pocket light is soaked; the damp batteries fail. There is another victim in the cellar, calling "*Mutti*," and it is his duty to find him and rescue him and drag him up to the light of day. He wades forward in the dark, and knows, in sleep, where it is no help to him, that the voice is his own.

Ernst, on his feet, stiff with the cold of a forgotten dream, makes a new decision. Everyone is lying; he will invent his own truth. Is it important if one-tenth of a lie is true? Is there a horror in a memory if it was only a dream? In Willi's shaving mirror now he wears the face that no superior officer, no prisoner, and no infatuated girl has ever seen. He will believe only what *he* knows. It is a great decision in an important day. Life begins with facts: he is Ernst Zimmermann, ex-Legionnaire. He has a ticket to Stuttgart. On the twenty-eighth of January, in the coldest winter since 1880, on the rue de Lille, in Paris, the child beaten by his mother cries for help and calls "*Maman, Maman.*"

O Lasting Peace

———————————— ■ ————————————

Though my Aunt Charlotte, my sad mother, my Uncle Theo,
and I all live together, and can see each other as often as we
need to, when Uncle Theo has something urgent to tell me he
comes here, to the Civic Tourist and Travel Bureau. He gets in
line, as if he were waiting to ask about the Bavarian Lakes and
Mountains Program or the Ludwig the Second Bus Circuit.
He slides close to the counter. I glance over, and suddenly
have to look down; Uncle Theo is so small he is always a surprise. He grins, scared to death of me. He is totally bald now,
not a hair to stretch sideways. He looks like a child's drawing
of two eyes and a smile. After a furtive trip to Berlin last

summer he edged along the queue to say he had called on my father, who is his brother and Aunt Charlotte's brother, too.

"Hilde, everything has gone wrong for him," said Uncle Theo, gripping the counter as if that might keep me from sending him away. "Do you remember how he couldn't stand cigarette smoke? How none of you could smoke when he was around?" Do I remember? It was one of the reasons my younger brother cleared out, leaving me to support half the household. "Well, *she* smokes all the time," said Uncle Theo. "She blows smoke in his face and so do her friends. She even eggs them on."

"Her friends," I repeated, writing it down. My expression was open but reserved. To anyone watching, Uncle Theo is supposed to be a client like any other.

"Low friends," said Uncle Theo. "Low Berliners in shady Berlin rackets. The kind of people who live in abandoned stores. No curtains, just whitewashed windows." At the word "shady" I did look as if I had seen my uncle somewhere before, but he is one more respectable survivor now, a hero of yesterday. "Ah, your poor father's kitchen," he went on lamenting. "Grease on the ceiling that deep," showing thumb and finger. "They're so down they've had to rent the parlour and the bedroom. They sleep on a mattress behind the front door."

"He's got what he wanted."

"Well, it had been going on between them for a long time, eh?" Embarrassment made him rise on his toes; it was almost a dance step. "After fifteen years she and your mother joined up and told him to choose. Your mother didn't understand what she was doing. She thought it was like some story on television."

My father left us five winters ago, at the age of sixty-three. I still have in mind the sight of my mother in a faint on the sofa and my Aunt Charlotte with an apron over her face, rocking and crying. I remember my Uncle Theo whispering into the telephone and my Aunt Charlotte taking the damp corner of her apron to wipe the leaves of the rubber plant. I came home from work on a dark evening to find this going on. I thought my Uncle Theo had been up to something. I went straight to my mother and gave her a shake. I was not frightened – she faints at will. I said, "Now you see what Uncle Theo is really like." She opened her eyes, sniffling. Her nylon chignon, which looks like a pound of butter sometimes, was askew on the pillow. She answered, "Be nice to poor Theo, he never had a wife to look after him." "Whose fault is that?" I said. I did not know yet that my father had gone, or even that such a thing might ever happen. Now it seems that my mother had been expecting it for fifteen years. A lifetime won't be enough to come to the end of their lies and their mysteries. I am the inspector, the governess, the one they tell stories to. And yet they depend on me! Without me they would be beggars, outcasts! Aunt Charlotte and my mother would wash windows in schoolhouses; they would haul buckets of dirty water up the stairs of office buildings; they would stand on vacant lots selling plastic combs and miniature Christmas trees!

My Uncle Theo began describing her – that other one. His face was as bright as if he were reciting a list of virtues: "I never did understand my brother. She has no taste, no charm, no looks, no culture, no education. She has a birthmark here," touching the side of his nose.

"I'm busy, Uncle Theo."

"We must send him money," he said, getting round to it.

"Well?" I said to the person next in line, over Uncle Theo's head.

"Hilde, we must send the poor old man money," he said, hanging on the counter. "A little every month, just the two of us." Uncle Theo thinks everyone else is old and poor. "Hilde – he's a night porter in a hospital. He doesn't like anything about the job. He can't eat the food."

Sometimes Uncle Theo will come here to intercede for our neighbours, having heard I have started legal action again. We have East German refugees in the next apartment – loud, boorish Saxons, six to a room. They send everything through the wall, from their coarse songs to their bedbugs. Long ago they were given a temporary housing priority, and then the city forgot them. The truth is these people live on priorities. They have wormed their way into everything. Ask anyone who it is that owns the laundries, the best farmlands, the electronics industry; you will always get the same answer: "East German refugees." At one time a popular riddle based on this subject went the rounds. Question: "Who were the three greatest magicians of all time?" Answer: "Jesus, because he turned water into wine. Hitler, because he turned Jews into soap. Adenauer, because he turned East German refugees into millionaires." Very few people can still repeat this without a mistake. Only two per cent of the readers of our morning paper still consider Hitler "a great figure." My own sister-in-law cannot say who Adenauer was, or what made him famous. As for Jesus, even I have forgotten what that particular miracle was about. A story that once made people laugh now brings nothing but "Who?" or "What?" or even "*Be careful.*" It is probably best not to try to remember.

At a quarter to two this Christmas Eve, my Uncle Theo turned up here again. The watchman was already dressed in his overcoat, standing by the glass doors with a bunch of keys in his hand. The banks, the grocers, the bookshops, the hairdressers were shut tight. The street outside looked dead, for those who weren't down with Asian flu were just getting over it. Uncle Theo slipped in past the porter. He wore his best winter pelisse with the seal collar and his seal hat. He looked smaller than ever, because of the great-coat and because of a huge brown paper parcel he was carrying. He made as if to come straight over, but I frowned and looked down. The cashier was on sick leave, too, and I was doing double duty. I knew the parcel was our Christmas goose. Uncle Theo buys one every year. Now, that he chooses well; it is not an imported Polish bird but a local goose, a fine one. I stood there counting money, twenty-five, thirty, fifty, and I heard Uncle Theo saying, "She is my niece." In my position I cannot murmur, "Oh, shut up," but I imagined him bound and trussed, like the goose, and with adhesive tape across his mouth. He was speaking to a man standing before him in the queue, a tall fellow wearing one of those square fur caps with ear flaps. The cap had certainly come from Russia. I guessed at once that the man was a showoff. Uncle Theo was telling him his history, of course, and probably mine as well – that I spoke four, or even seven, languages and that the tourist office could not manage without me. What a waste of time, and how foolish of Uncle Theo!

Even from behind the counter I could see the showoff's wedding ring. None of the staff was happy. We were almost the only people still working in the whole city. It was one of the days when you can smell the central heating, like an aluminum saucepan burning. I looked sharply at Hausen, my assistant. He has devised a way of reading a newspaper in a desk drawer, folded in quarters. He can even turn the pages, with movements so economical only I can see them. You would never guess that he was reading – he seems to be looking for pencils. "Take some of these people over, will you?" I called out. Hausen didn't respond, and the line didn't move. Uncle Theo's voice was now clear: "I also happened to be in Calcutta when the end of the world was expected. That was February 5, 1962. The Calcutta stock exchange closed down. People left their homes and slept in tents. Imagine – the stock exchange affected. Everyone waiting. Eminent persons, learned professors." Uncle Theo shook his head.

"You were there on business, I suppose," said the man in the square cap. He had to stand in profile so they could go on talking. It made an untidy sort of queue. Uncle Theo looked ridiculous. The pelisse swamps him.

"No, no. I was retired long ago," he said. "Forcibly retired. My factories were bombed. I made a little porcelain – pretty stuff. But my vocation was elsewhere." Having let that sink in, he put on his quotations voice and said, "'And now, like many another wreck, I am throwing myself into the arms of literature.' I found much to inspire me in India. The holy men. The end of the world on February 5, 1962. The moon. The moon in India has no phases. It is full all the year round."

In a job like mine it would be best not to have relatives at all. Nothing of Uncle Theo's is quite the truth or entirely a lie. The remark about the moon was a mistake, caused by his lack of schooling. For "factories" he meant "one workroom," and for "porcelain" he meant "hand-painted ashtrays." It is true about the literature, though. Two of his poems have been set to music and sung by our choral society. "In Autumn, in Summer, in Autumn, in Summer," with the voices fading on the last word, is not without effect. The other, which begins, "O peace, O peace, O lasting peace, / We all demand a lasting peace," is less successful. It sounds preachy, even when sung in a lively way.

"Will someone please take over these people," I said, this time loud enough so that Hausen couldn't pretend not to hear. The whole queue shuffled obediently to the left – all but the last two. These were Uncle Theo and his new friend, of course. The friend made for me and put a traveller's cheque down on the counter. I looked at it. It had been signed "F. T. Gellner" and countersigned "F. Thomas Gellner." Haste, carelessness, perhaps. But the "T" on the top line was a printer's capital, while the second was written in script. I pushed the cheque back with one finger: "Sorry, it's not the same signature."

He pretended not to see what I meant, then said, "Oh, that. I can cross out the 'Thomas' and put the initial on, can't I?"

"Not on a traveller's. Next person, please," I said, even though the next was Uncle Theo, who had no business here.

"I'll write a personal cheque," said the man, getting a pen out first.

"This is not a bank," I said. "We cash traveller's as a favour to clients."

"But the banks are closed."

"Yes," I said. "It is Christmas Eve. It isn't only the 'Thomas,' but also your capitals. The two signatures are absolutely not the same."

"Is that all?" he cried out, so happily (thinking it was settled) that even deaf Hausen looked over. "I write one way sometimes, then another. Let me show you – my driver's license, my passport . . ." He started tumbling papers out of an inside pocket. "I should be more careful," he said to me, trying to play at being friends.

"It is not my business to examine your driver's license," I said. "The two signatures are not the same."

He looked round the office and said, "Isn't there anyone else I can see?"

"It is Christmas Eve," I said, "and I am in charge. The manager is at home with Asian flu. Would you like his number?"

Uncle Theo stuck his head out sideways, like a little boiled egg with a hat on it, and said, "I can vouch for the gentleman." He must have forgotten who and where he was. "I can sign anything you like," he said. "My name is important locally."

"There is nothing to sign and I do not need your name." Important locally? Where is his name? On the war memorial? Have they called a street after him? His name is not even on a civil registry – he never married, even though there has been a shortage of husbands since Bismarck.

The man took no more notice of Uncle Theo; he had finally understood that the honourary assistant head of the choral society was of no use to anyone. To be rid of the incident, I said, "Sign another traveller's in my presence."

"That was my last one."

Uncle Theo repeated, "I can vouch for the gentleman. I have seen the gentleman buying in shops – spending," said my uncle, making a circle of his thumb and forefinger for emphasis under the brown paper parcel, as if we were poor villagers for whom the very sight of money was a promise of honour.

"Ask your hotel to cash a cheque," I said. "I'm sorry but I cannot deal with you any longer. It is Christmas Eve."

"I'm not in a hotel. I mean that I am staying here with friends." Of course, I had seen the "friends." She was waiting outside, trying to seem casual, wearing one of those reddish fur coats. Snow fell on her hair.

"Ask your friends to lend you something."

"You could save me that embarrassment," he said, trying for friendliness again.

"It is not my business to save you embarrassment," I said, glancing at his wedding ring.

Even when he had got as far as the door, and the watchman was preparing to lock it behind him, he kept looking back at me. I made a point of being taken up by Uncle Theo, who now stood woebegone and scuffing his feet, shifting his burden from arm to arm.

"That wasn't kind, Hilde," he began. "The poor man – he'll have a sad Christmas."

"Be quick, Uncle Theo. What do you want?"

"Tonight," he said, "when we are eating our dinner, and the candles are lighted on the Christmas tree . . ."

"Yes?"

"Try not to cry. Let the girls enjoy themselves. Don't think of sad things." The girls are my mother and Aunt Charlotte.

"What else is there?" I said. I could have piled all our sad Christmases on the counter between us – the Christmas when I was thirteen and we were firebombed, and saved nothing except a knife and fork my mother had owned when she was little. She still uses them; "Traudi" is engraved on the handle of each. It worries my mother to find anything else next to her plate. It makes her feel as if no one considered her – as if she were devalued in her own home. I remember another Christmas and my father drinking wine with Uncle Theo; wine slowed him down, we had to finish his sentences for him. They say that when he left us he put an apple in his pocket. My Aunt Charlotte packed some of his things afterward and deposited them with a waiter he knew. The next Christmas, my Uncle Theo, the only man of the house now, drank by himself and began to caper like a little goat, round and round the tree. I looked at the table, beautifully spread with a starched cloth, and I saw four large knives and forks, as for four enormous persons. Aunt Charlotte had forgotten about my mother.

"Oh, my own little knife and fork, I can't see them!" cried my mother, coming in at that moment, in blue lace down to her ankles.

"Oh, my own little arse," said Uncle Theo, in my mother's voice, still dancing.

He was just as surprised as we were. He stared all round to see who could have said such a thing. My mother locked herself in her room. My Aunt Charlotte tapped on the door and said, "We only want you to eat a little compote, dear Traudi."

"Then you will have to bring it here," said my mother. But after saying that, she would not open the door. We knew she would come out in time to watch *The Nutcracker Suite*, and so we left the house, pretending we were about to pay our Christmas visits a day early. We sat in the railway station for a long time, as if we were waiting for someone. When we came back, we found she had put the short chain lock on the front door of the apartment, so that all the keys in the world wouldn't let you in. Here we were, all three wearing hats, and hoping our neighbours would not peep out to see who was doing all the ringing. Finally someone did emerge – a grubby little boy. Behind him we could see a large party round a table, looking out and laughing at us, with their uneducated mouths wide open. We said courteously that our relative must have fallen asleep and, being slightly deaf, could not hear the doorbell.

"We knew there must be a deaf person in that apartment," said someone at the table.

"There is no Christmas in India," said Uncle Theo, becoming one of their party. "It has no meaning there." I was glad to see that my aunt and I looked decent. "My sister-in-law once had a great emotional shock," said Uncle Theo, accepting a glass. "Christmas is so sad."

A gust of feeling blew round the table. Yes, Christmas is sad. Everyone has a reason for jumping out the window at Christmas and in the spring. Meanwhile I was calling our number, and I could hear our telephone ringing on the other side of the wall.

The neighbours' wallpaper is covered with finger marks, like my
sister-in-law's. "Why not send for the police?" someone said.
My aunt looked as if she wanted to throw an apron over her
face and cry, which was all she did when her own brother left.
"Well, Uncle?" I said. Everyone looked at the man who had
been to India. Before he could decide, the little boy who
had opened the door said, "I can get round by the balconies."
Do you see how easy it is for these people to spy on us? They
must have done it hundreds of times. All he had to do was
straddle the partition between the two balconies, which he did,
knocking down the flowerpots covered with squares of plastic
for the winter. My aunt frowned at me, as if to say it didn't
matter. He cupped his hands round his eyes, peering through
the panes of the double glass doors. Then he pounded with
both fists, breathing hard, his cheeks as red as if they had been
slapped. "The lady is just sitting on the floor watching television," he said finally.

"Stone-deaf," said Uncle Theo, keeping up the story.

"She is dead," wailed my aunt. "My sister-in-law has had
a stroke."

"Break the panes," I cried to the child. "Use a flowerpot. Be
careful not to cut yourself." I was thinking of blood on the
parquet floor.

She was not dead, of course, but only sulking and waiting
for *The Nutcracker Suite*. She said she had fainted. We helped
her to an armchair. It was difficult after that to turn the
neighbours out, and even harder to return to our original
status; they would stop us on the stairs and ask for news of

"the poor sick lady." A year was needed to retreat to "Good morning," and back again to nothing but an inclination of the head. For although we put lighted candles in the windows on Christmas Eve as a reminder of German separation, it seems very different when masses of refugees move in next door, six to a room, and entirely without culture. It would be good to have everyone under one flag again, but the Saxons in Saxony, et cetera, please.

With all this behind me, the Christmas memories of my life, what could I say except "What else is there?"

"Try not to think at all," said Uncle Theo, grinning with nervousness and his anxious little bandit's eyes darting everywhere. "Bandit" is perhaps too much; he never had a gram of civic feeling, let us say. "I have tickets to *The Gypsy Baron*," he said. So that was what he had come to tell me!

"What do you mean, Uncle Theo?"

"For the four of us, the day after Christmas."

"Out of the question," I said.

"Now, why, Hilde? The girls like music."

"Use your head, Uncle Theo. I can't talk now."

What did he mean, *why?* It was out of the question, that was all. First, the flu epidemic. People were coughing and sneezing without covering their faces.

"I wanted you to have two days to think it over," said Uncle Theo. He gave me the impression that he was sliding, crawling. I don't know why he is so afraid of me.

It seemed so evident: it is wrong to take them out to the theatre, or anywhere in the cold. It disturbs their habits. They are perfectly happy with their television. They have their own warm little theatre in our parlour. My mother is always allowed to choose the program, as you may imagine. She settles in with a bowl of walnuts on her lap. My aunt never sees the beginning of anything, because she walks round examining her plants. She sits down finally, and the others tell her the plot, when there is one. Uncle Theo drinks white wine and laughs at everything. One by one they fall asleep in their chairs. I wake them up and send them off to bed while the late news predicts the next day's weather. Why drive them out in the cold to see an operetta? And then, how are we supposed to get there? The car has been put away for the winter, with the insurance suspended and the battery disconnected. Say that we get it out and in running order – where does Uncle Theo expect me to park? I suppose I might go earlier in the day, on foot, and pick out the streets near the theatre where parking might be allowed. Or we could *all* go very early and sit in the car until the theatre opens. But we would have to keep the engine running and the heater on, and we would be certain to have blinding headaches within the hour. We might walk, but these old persons get terribly warm in their overcoats, and then they perspire and catch chills and fever. I am surprised that the city is letting the play be produced at this time.

All this I explained to Uncle Theo in the calmest voice imaginable.

He said, "I had better turn the tickets in."

"Why?" I said. "Why do that? As you say, the girls like music. Why deprive them of an outing? I only want you to realize, for once, the possible results of your actions."

Why is it that everyone is depressed by hearing the truth? I tell the office manager about Hausen reading newspapers in a desk drawer. His face puckers. He wishes I had never brought it up. He looks out the window; he has decided to forget it. He will forget it. I have never said a thing; he is not obliged to speak to Hausen, let alone sack him. When my brother married a girl with a chin like a Turkish slipper, I warned him what his children would be like – that he would be ashamed to have them photographed because of their ugly faces.

I say to my mother, "How can you giggle over nothing? One son was killed, the other one never comes to see you, and your husband left you for another woman at the age of sixty-three." Half an hour later, unless someone has hurt her feelings, or changed the television program without asking, she has forgotten her own life's story. The family say Uncle Theo is a political hero, but isn't he just a man who avoided going to war? He was called up for military service after Stalingrad. At the medical examination he pointed out his age, his varicose veins, his blood pressure, but none of that helped. He was fit for service – for the next wholesale offering, in Uncle Theo's view. He put on his clothes, still arguing, and was told to take a file with his name on it to a room upstairs. It was on his way up that he had his revelation. Everything concerning his person

was in that file. If the file disappeared, then Uncle Theo did,
too. He turned and walked straight out the front door. He did
not destroy the file, in case they should come round asking; he
intended to say he had not understood the instructions. No
one came, and soon after this his workroom was bombed and
the file became ashes. When Uncle Theo was arrested it was
for quite another reason, having to do with black-market
connections. He went first to prison, then, when the jail was
bombed, to a camp. Here he wore on his striped jacket the
black sleeve patch that meant "anti-social." It is generally
thought that he wore the red patch, meaning "political." As
things are now, it gives him status. But it was not so at the
time, and he himself has told me that the camp was run by that
anti-social element. It was they who had full control of the
internal order, the margarine racket, the extra-soup racket,
the cigarette traffic. Uncle Theo was there less than a month,
all told, but it changed his outlook for life.

Now consider my situation: eighteen years with the Civic
Tourist and Travel Bureau, passed over for promotion because
I am female, surrounded at home by aged children who can't
keep their own histories straight. They have no money, no
property, no future, no recorded past, nothing but secrets. My
parents never explained themselves. For a long time I thought
they kept apple juice in our cellar locker. After my father left
us I went down and counted eighteen bottles of white wine.
Where did it come from? "Tell me the truth," I have begged
them. "Tell me everything you remember." They sit smiling
and sipping wine out of postwar glasses. My mother cracks

walnuts and passes the bowl around. That is all I have for an answer.

Sometimes on my way home I take the shortcut through the cemetery. The long bare snowy space is where Russian prisoners used to be buried. When the bodies were repatriated, even the gravestones were taken – all but two. Perhaps the families forgot to claim the bodies; or perhaps they were not really prisoners but impostors of some kind. Whatever the reason, two fairly clean stones stand alone out of the snow, with nothing around them. Nearby are the graves of Russian prisoners from the 1914 war. The stones are old and dark and tipped every way. The more I think of it the more I am certain those two could not have been Russians.

Yesterday in the cemetery, at six o'clock, there were lovers standing motionless, like a tree. I had to step off the path; snow came over the tops of my boots. I saw candles burning in little hollows on some of the graves, and Christmas trees on the graves of children. What shall I do when I have to bury the family? Uncle Theo speaks of buying a plot, but in the plot he has in mind there is no room for me and he knows it. I should have married, and when I died I'd be buried with my in-laws – that is what Uncle Theo says to himself. When you speak about dying he looks confused. His face loses its boiled-egg symmetry. Then he says, "Cheer up, Hilde, it can't be so bad or they would have found a way to stop it by now."

He was a guard in the prisoner-of-war camp. I forgot to mention that. In fact that was how he got out of his own camp; they were so desperate that they asked for volunteers from among the anti-social element – the thieves, the pimps, the black-marketeers. Most of them went to the Eastern front and died there. Uncle Theo, undersized and elderly, became a guard not too far from home. Even there he got on well, and when the Russian prisoners broke out at the end, they did not hang him or beat him to death but simply tied him to a tree. They told him a phrase he was to repeat phonetically if Russian troops got there before the others. Luckily for him the Americans turned up first; all he has ever been able to say in a foreign language is "*Pro domo sua,*" and he must have learned that phonetically, too. He hardly went to school. Uncle Theo was able to prove he had once been arrested, and that turned out to be in his favour. Now he has a pension, and is considered a hero, which is annoying. He was never a member of any party. He does not go to church. "*Pro domo sua,*" he says, closing an eye.

Uncle Theo applied for war reparations in 1955. He offered his record – destruction of porcelain factory, unjust imprisonment, pacifist convictions, humane and beloved guard in prisoner-of-war camp – and in 1960 he received a lump sum and a notice of a pension to follow. He immediately left for India, with a touring group composed mostly of little widows. But he decided not to marry any of them. He brought us a scarf apiece and a set of brass bowls. It was after his return that he wrote "O Lasting Peace."

One last thing: without my consent, without even asking me, Uncle Theo advertised for a husband for me. This was years ago, before he had his pension. He gave my age as "youthful," my face and figure as "gracious," my world outlook as "modern," and my upbringing as "delicate." There was too much unemployment at the time, and so no one answered. Eleven years later he ran the same notice, without changing a word. The one person who answered was invited – by Uncle Theo – to call and see if he wanted me. I saw the candidate through a fog of shame. I remember his hair, which sprang from his forehead in a peculiar way, like black grass, and that he sat with his feet turned in and the toe of one shoe over the other. He was not really a fool, but only strange, like all persons who do not really intend to go through with the wedding. My aunt, my mother, and my uncle stated my qualities for me and urged him to eat fruitcake. My mother had to say, "Hilde has been so many years with the tourist office that we can't even count them," which knocked out the "youthful" bit, even if he had been taken in by it. It was a few days after a Christmas; fresh candles were lighted on the tree. The candidate turned his head, swallowing. Everyone wanted him to say something. "Won't the curtains catch fire?" he asked. I'm sure Uncle Theo would have picked up the tree and moved it if he had been able, he was that excited by his guest. Then the man finished eating his cake and went away, and I knew we would not hear about him again; and that was a good riddance.

"You are so anxious to have this apartment to yourselves," I said to my family. "You have made yourselves cheap over a peasant who sits with one foot on the other. How would you pay the rent here without me? Don't you understand that I can't leave you?" At the same time, I wanted to run out on the balcony screaming "Come back!" but I was afraid of knocking the flowerpots over. I've forgotten why I wanted to mention this.

An Alien Flower

───────■───────

My daughter wept when the news reached us here in Cologne that Bibi had died. It was the first loss by death she had ever experienced, except for that of our old brown poodle, and it affected her to the point of fantasy. She accused me of having murdered Bibi; of having treated her like a servant; of having been jealous of her brains and her beauty (her beauty?); and, finally, of having driven her out of our house with my capricious demands, my moods, and my coldness.

Everyone knows what it is like now to be judged by spoiled, ignorant children. Of course we never considered Bibi a servant! That is a pure invention. From the very beginning – when we

were, in fact, her employers – she ate at our table and called us
Julius and Helga. There were hundreds of thousands of girls
like Bibi in those days, just as poor and alone. No person was
ever considered to blame for his own poverty or solitude. You
would never have dreamed of hinting it could be his own fault.
You never knew what that person's past might be, or what
unspoken grudge he might be hiding. There was also a joint
past that lay all around us in heaps of charred stone. The
streets still smelled of terror and ashes, particularly after rain.
Every stone held down a ghost, or a frozen life, or a dreadful
secret. No one was inferior, because everyone was. A social
amnesty had been declared.

Bibi must have been in her early twenties then. She was a
refugee, from Silesia. In the town she named as her birthplace
everyone had died or run away. She had no friends, no family,
and no money, but she must have been given some sort of education at one time, because she had been accepted in high
school here, in the terminal class. How she got in is a mystery.
There was no room for anyone, and students were selected like
grains of sand. People of all ages were trying to go to school –
middle-aged men, prisoners of war coming back and claiming
an education. In those days, so many papers and documents
had been burned that people like Bibi could say anything they
liked about themselves. Still, she had passed some sort of
entrance examination – she must have. She had also found a
place to live, and she supported herself doing sewing and
ironing and minding babies – whatever she could find. We had
her Tuesday, Thursday, and Saturday, for housework; three
evenings a week. Her dinner was part of her wages, but as the

evening meal was nothing but soup she did not have to give up her ration tickets. After she had been with us for a while, one of her teachers told Julius that Bibi was brilliant. Yes, brilliant. Without any real culture, without . . . But brilliant all the same. As soon as Julius was certain it was true, he found a part-time job for Bibi in the first research laboratory they were establishing then at Possner. Possner was looking for bright young people with a promising future and no past. It was an incredible stroke of fortune for someone in Bibi's situation. She stayed at Possner on that part-time basis until she published her thesis in 1955. (Possner sent her to the university.) After that she went on to a much, much better job. From the time she met Julius, Bibi had nothing but luck.

Her thesis was called "The Occurrence of Alkaloids in the" – in the something. In a word beginning with "A." I could look it up – there must be twelve copies or even more down in the wine cellar. "The Occurrence" was nearly a book – eighty-two pages long, not counting the pages of thanks and the dedications. Julius has a whole page to himself: "To Doctor Engineer Julius Lauer, of the firm of Possner (Cologne), my Heartfelt Gratitude." The copies are well bound in that brown paper that imitates bark. Possner must have paid.

Bibi was something of a friend, finally. My daughter called her Aunt and was taught to respect her. She even lived with us for a time – for ten years in our old house, and for several months in the house we have now. She emigrated to an American branch of Possner and she died over there.

I don't think she ever wanted to marry. She never mentioned it. She had peculiar opinions and was no good at hiding what she thought. After the age of thirty she became insistent. She would insist on the same thing over and over – usually something to do with the harsh side of life. She felt shy about some ugly scars she had on her legs, and wore thick stockings even in summer, and would never go on a beach.

Even if I had ever considered Bibi less than myself, how could I have shown it? By having her eat in the kitchen alone? In the days when we met Bibi the kitchen was a privileged place, the only warm room anyone had. Julius worked nearly every evening then and I was glad to have Bibi's company. As she sewed and ironed I sat nearby, reading, sometimes talking to her, wishing she would stop whistling and singing but not liking to say so. She had several odious habits. For instance, she owned only one pair of stockings and was afraid of wearing them out. As soon as she arrived she would take them off and drape them over the back of a chair. Once, Heidi, the old brown poodle we had, licked Bibi's bare legs under the table.

"Heidi, you swine!" Bibi wailed. I have forgotten to say how funny she looked and sounded when she was young. She had short blond hair that stuck out like stiff flower petals, and she spoke with a coarse, droll, regional accent that turned her simplest remarks into comedy. "Heidi, you swine," became a joke between Julius and me until the day he was informed she was brilliant. After that, I lost my bearings where Bibi was concerned, for now she was part of Possner, and Possner was also Julius, and neither Julius nor Possner was to be laughed at. Possner was a small industrial complex then – nothing compared with a great house such as Bayer; but to Julius it was a new force in the nation, an élite army for which he enlisted the best of recruits. Julius was, I suppose, a lieutenant in the industry-army. He knew he would go up and up as this new army grew. I knew it too, and that was why I had asked for help – why I had Bibi. I was afraid that if I became a house-wife Julius would find me dull and would leave me behind. Every morning, instead of scrubbing and dusting, I read a newspaper. The papers were thin; the news was boring and censored, or, rather, "approved." I would begin at the back, with the deaths and the cinema advertisements, and work forward to the political news. In the afternoon I walked Heidi and tried to read books belonging to Julius. Of that period of my "education" I remember long, sleepy winter afternoons, and I see myself trying to keep awake. I also spent hours in queues, because meat, clothing, and even matches were hard to find.

Like Bibi, I had no friends; I had no family, except Julius. I was not from Cologne but from Dortmund. Anyone who had ever known me or loved me had been killed in one period of seven weeks. I was a year or two older than Bibi – about twenty-four. I was not as pretty as my daughter is now, though my wedding picture shows me with soft chestnut hair. In the picture I look as though someone had just scolded me. I was nervous in those days and easily startled. I worried about gas escaping, burglars at the windows, and bicycles ridden by drunken criminals; I was also afraid of being thought too stupid for Julius and unworthy of being his wife.

I can still see us in our kitchen, under the faintest of light bulbs, with three plates of soup on the table and a plate for Heidi, the poodle, on the floor. Heidi had belonged to Julius's parents. "Four old survivors," said Julius, though Heidi was old and we three were young.

Julius was made a captain and we took our first holiday. We went to Rome. I remember a long train journey during which we ate hard-boiled-egg sandwiches and slept in our clothes. The shops dazzled me; I wanted to buy presents for dozens of people, but I had only Bibi. I chose a marble darning egg and a pair of sandals that were the wrong size. I had thought of her feet as enormous, but to my surprise they were narrow and fine. She could not take two steps in the new sandals without sliding. She kept the shoes as a souvenir. Julius found them in her trunk, wrapped in white tissue paper, after she died.

A change in Bibi's status came at about that time. Julius had wangled an excellent scholarship for her. With that, and the money she earned at Possner, Bibi could afford an apartment. She said she was happy as she was, but Julius wanted Possner employees to live decently. Also, she roomed with a family of refugees, and Julius did not want her to waste her mental energies talking about the tides of history. I can truthfully say that Julius has never discussed historical change. Do leaves speak? Are mountains asked to have an opinion? Bibi still resisted, saying there was no such thing as a flat in Cologne; but Julius found one. He personally moved her to her new quarters – one room, gas ring, and sink. Just about what she was leaving, except that now she lived alone. I don't know how the room was furnished – Bibi never invited me to see it. She still came to us for three weekly evenings of housework, still ate her

bread and soup and put the money we paid her aside. We were
astonished at the size of her savings account when we saw her
bankbook years later.

Julius was not so much concerned with Bibi as with Possner.
When he helped other people it was because he was helping
the firm. His life was his work; his faith was in Possner's future.
I believed in Julius. In one of the books belonging to him – the
books that gave me so much trouble on winter afternoons – I
read that belief, like love, could not be taken by storm. I knew
that Julius lied sometimes, but so do all divinities. Divinities
invented convenient fables and they appeared in strange dis-
guises, but they were never mistaken. I believed, because he
said it, that we would not live among ashes forever, and that
he would give me a new, beautiful house. Because he vouched
for Bibi's genius I had to believe in it too. It was my duty to
imagine Bibi ten years from now with a Nobel Prize for chemistry. This was another Bibi, tall and gracious and speaking
pure German. She had stopped singing tunes from *The Merry
Wives of Windsor* in such an annoying way, she no longer sat
like an elephant or laughed with her mouth wide open or held
bread on the palm of her hand to spread it with margarine.

If, in this refined and comfortable future, I corrected Bibi's
manners it was a sign that the postwar social amnesty could
not go on. In fact, the rules of difference were restored long
before the symphony orchestras were full strength, the prisoners were home, the schools were rebuilt. Seeing where Bibi
was going, I began wondering where she had started out. Her
name, Beate Brüning, was honest and plain. She hinted that
once she had not lived like other people and had missed some

of her schooling on that account. Why? Had she been ill, or delinquent? Was she, as well as Silesian, slightly foreign? Sometimes male ancestors had been careless about the women they married. Perhaps Bibi had been unable to give a good account of herself. My textbook of elementary biology in high school explained about the pure and the impure, beginning with plant life. Here was the picture of an upright, splendid, native plant, and next to it the photograph of a spindly thing that never bloomed and that was in some way an alien flower. Bibi's round face, her calm eyes, her expression of sweetness and anxiety to please spoke of nothing but peasant sanity; still, she was different; she was "other." She never mentioned her family or said how they had died. I could only guess that they must have vanished in the normal way of a recent period – killed at the front, or lost without trace in the east, or burned alive in air raids. Who were the Brünings? Was she ashamed of them? Were they Socialists, radicals, troublemakers, black-marketeers, prostitutes, wife-beaters, informers, Witnesses of Jehovah? After she died no one came forward to claim her bank account, though Julius was scrupulous about advertising. Whoever the Brünings were, Bibi was their survivor, and she was as pure as the rest of us in the sense that she was alone, swept clean of friends and childhood myths and of childhood itself. But someone, at some time, must have existed and must have called her Bibi. A diminutive is not a thing you invent for yourself.

Of course, my life was not composed of these long specula-tions, but of sub-themes, common questions and answers. One day new information about Julius came into my hands. As I

stood on a chair to fetch a pair of bedsheets down from the
high shelf of a cupboard, a folded blanket and an old jacket
belonging to him came slipping down on top of me. I clutched
at the edge of the shelf to steady myself and had under my
fingers someone's diary. Still standing on the chair, I let the
diary fall open. I read how Julius and an unknown girl –
the writer of the diary – had pushed the girl's bed close to a
window one sunny winter afternoon. "No one could see us,"
the girl felt obliged to note, as if she were writing for some
other person. A bombed wall outlined in snow was their only
neighbour. The sky was winter blue.

Now I am free was my first thought, but what did I mean? I
wanted to live with Julius, not without him. I did not know
what I meant.

I remembered the new, beautiful house he had promised,
with the clock from Holland, the wallpaper from France,
the swimming-pool tiles from Italy. I sat down and read the
diary through.

On the girl's birthday Julius took her to a restaurant, but
friends "connected with him professionally" came in. After
twisting and turning and trying to hide his face, Julius sent her
to the ladies' room with instructions to wait there for five
minutes and then go home without stopping to speak to him.
"What a bad ending for an evening that began with such
promise," the diarist remarked. Did she live in Cologne? "Two
nights," she recorded, or "one afternoon," or "one and one-
half hours," followed by "did everything," then "everything,"
then finally just the initial of the word, as if she herself were no
longer surprised or enchanted. One dull lonely weekend when

she had not seen Julius for days, she wrote, "The sun is shining on all the rooftops and filling every heart with gladness while I   Over the rooftops the sun shines but I   My heart is sad though the sun is filling every heart . . ."

"Helga, are you all right?"

Here was Bibi breaking in – anxious, good, and extremely comic. Her accent would have made even tragedy seem hilarious, I thought then. I began to laugh, and blurted out, "Julius has always had other women, but now he leaves their belongings where I can find them." Bibi's look of shock was on my behalf. ". . . always had women," I repeated. "I said I didn't mind." The truth was that each time had nearly killed me. Also, the girls were poor things, sometimes barely literate. Looking down at the diary on my lap I thought, Well, at least this one can spell, and I am his wife, and he treats me with consideration, and he has promised me a house.

"Oh, Helga," Bibi cried, kneeling and clutching my hands, "you have always been kind to me." She muttered something else. I made her repeat it. "I don't understand; I don't keep that sort of a diary" was what Bibi had said.

So in the same hour I found out about Bibi and Julius too. Here was my situation: I was pregnant, and I should not have been standing on a chair to begin with. I was ill. I had such violent spasms sometimes that Julius would ask if I was trying to vomit the baby. I had absolutely no one but Julius, and nowhere to go. Moreover, as I have said, I did not *want* to live without him. As for Bibi, when I was feeling at my most wretched she was the only person the smell of whose skin and hair did not turn my stomach. I could not stand the scent of soap, or cologne, or food cooking, or milk, or smoke, or other people. Bibi looked after me. Once she said shyly, "I know, I know that mixture of hunger and nausea, when all you long for is good white bread." I remember sweating and trembling and thinking that it was she, it was Bibi, who was the good white bread. I never hated Bibi. I may have pitied her. I knew a little about Julius and I had a fear of explosions. I could have said to Julius, "I know about Bibi and you." What next? Bibi then departs and Julius and I are alone. He knows I know, which means we live in ruins and ashes forever. All I could feel was Bibi's utter misery; I saw her stricken face, her rough hands, and then I began to cry too, and we two – we two grown-up war orphans – dried each other's tears. I am quite certain Bibi never knew I had understood.

It was Bibi who saw me into the clinic where Roma was born. Julius was in Belgium. I asked Bibi to send him a telegram concerning the baby's name. "I want Roma because that was where she was conceived," I told her. "Don't put *conceived* in the telegram. Julius will understand."

She nodded and said something in her ridiculous accent and went out the door. In a sense I never saw her again; I mean that this was the last I saw of a certain young, good-hearted Bibi. Julius came back before receiving the telegram; perhaps she hadn't sent it. It was two days before I remembered to ask about Bibi, and another before she was found. She had taken gardénal. She was alive, but she had been in a long, untended coma. The flesh on her legs had begun to alter, and she had to stay for a long time in the hospital – the hospital where Roma was born – after her skin-graft operations. That was why she wore thick stockings forever after, even in summer.

No one told me, at first. Julius made up a story. He said Bibi had met a young engineer and had run away with him. It sounded unlike her, but it was also unlike him to be so inventive, so I thought it must be true. I sat up against a starched pillowcase Bibi had brought me from home, and I invited Julius to admire Roma's hands and feet. He said that Bibi's lover was named Wolfgang, and we laughed and thought of Bibi on her wedding night saying, "Wolfgang, you swine!"

All Bibi was ever able to explain to me later was that somewhere between my room and the front door of the hospital she had asked God to strike her with lightning. She stood still and counted up to ten; ten seconds was the limit she gave Him to prove He could hear. Nothing happened. She saw a rubbery begonia on a windowsill; an aide pushing along a trolley of tea mugs; a father and two children waiting on a bench with the patience of the ignorant. She could not recall whether or not she had ever sent the telegram. She next remembered being at home, in the room Julius had insisted would be in keeping with her new position, and that there she had taken gardénal. The gardénal was in the form of large flat tablets, like salt pills. She said she had "always" had them, even in her refugee camp. For someone who had access to every sort of modern poison at Possner, she had chosen an old-fashioned, feminine way of death. She broke up the tablets patiently, one after the other, sitting on the edge of her bed. She was obliged to swallow so much water that she began to be sick on it, and finally she heated a little milk on the gas ring. The milk probably saved her.

She had imagined dying would be like a slow anesthetic; she thought death could be inhaled, like fresh air. But it was a black cloak being blown down on one, she told me – like a cape slipping off a hook and falling in soft folds over your hands and face.

By the time Bibi was well enough to tell me these things, Julius had forgotten her, and had all but forgotten me. He was in love with no one but Roma, a baby ten days old, named for a holiday. This was a quiet love affair that gave us all a period of relative peace. I don't believe he visited Bibi once, though he paid for her private room, the skin-graft operations, and her long convalescence. Bibi begged to be put in a ward, for being alone made her feel miserable, but Julius refused. She finally came home to us, because I needed someone; my health had broken down. I had fits of crying so prolonged that my eyelids became allergic to daylight and I had to spend hours lying down in the dark. Bibi worked part time at Possner, looked after Roma, ran the house, and saw that I was allowed to recover very, very slowly.

Julius was now a major, and we moved into the first of our new, beautiful homes. We had a room for Bibi, next to Roma's. She kept that room for ten years and never once made a change in it. She would not admit any furniture except a bed, a wardrobe, a small bookcase that served as her night table, and a lamp. She did not correspond with anyone. Her books, concerned with one subject, were called *Tetrahedron Letters*, *The Chemistry of Steroids*, *Steroid Reactions*, and so on. I tried to read her thesis but I could not take in ". . . washed repeatedly in a solution of bicarbonate of soda, then in distilled water, and dried on sulphate of sodium. After evaporation, a residue of 8.78 . . ." I discovered that she kept a journal, but it told me nothing. "Monday – Conversation with Arab student in canteen. Interesting." "Tuesday – *Funtumia latifolia* is a tree in Western Africa. Flowers white. Wood white. Used for matches, fruit crates." "Wednesday – Heidi dead." "Thursday – Roma draws Papa, Mama, Aunt Bibi, self, a tombstone for Heidi. Accept drawing as gift." "Friday – Menses." "Saturday – Allied Powers forbid demonstration against rearmament." "Sunday – Visit kennel. New puppy for Roma. Roma undecided." This was Bibi's journal in a typical week.

Bibi had no sense of beauty. It was impossible to make her room attractive or interesting, and I avoided showing it to strangers. She never left a towel or a toothbrush in the bathroom she and Roma shared. I sometimes wondered if she had been raised in an orphanage, where every other bed held a potential thief. All her life she used only the smallest amount of water. At first, when she washed dishes I could never persuade her to rinse them. Water was something to be rationed, but I never learned why. She could keep a cake of soap or a tube of toothpaste for months. She wanted to live owning nothing, using nothing. On the other hand, once an object had come into her hands, and if she did not give it away immediately, to be parted from it later on was anguish. Sometimes I took her handbag and dumped it upside down. I would get rid of the broken comb, the thumbed mirror, the pencil stubs, and replace all this rubbish with something clean and new. But she was miserable until everything became old, cracked, and "hers" again. Most refugees talked too much. Bibi said too little, and that in disturbing fragments. Drink went straight to her head. At our parties I looked out for her, and when I saw the bad signs – her eyes pressed to slits, her head thrown back, a trusting smile – I would take her glass away. Once, during a dinner party, her voice floated over the rest of the talk: "Some adolescents, under difficult circumstances, were instructed in algebra and physics by distinguished professors. A gypsy girl named Angela, who had been in a concentration camp, was taught to read and write by a woman doctor of philosophy whose husband had been shot in the cellar of a prison in Moscow in 1941."

After that, I came to a quiet agreement with Julius that Bibi be given nothing to drink except when we were alone. I could not expect Julius's guests to abandon their own homes and their own television to hear nothing but disjointed anecdotes. This was the year when every television network celebrated the anniversary of the liberation of the concentration camps. Roma sat on a low stool with her elbows on her knees and saw everything. We now had a fifth person in the family, a young man from Possner named Michael. Julius had brought him in. Michael must already have decided to marry Julius's daughter if only he could remain important to Julius while Roma was growing up. I noticed that he thought Aunt Bibi was also someone who had to be pleased. In a way, Michael was a new kind of Bibi. The firm intended to send him to an advanced course in business management, just as Bibi had been sent to the university.

Michael was trying to take the political temper of the house. He would stand up and sit down and seem alternately interested in Roma's television program and wretchedly uneasy. He wondered if he would bother the three older people by too much attention to the screen, or lose Roma forever by not showing enough interest. Roma was so young then that Michael, at twenty-two, must have seemed like a parent. Bibi sat reading a speech Julius was to make at a congress where English would be the working language. From time to time she glanced at the screen, then went on making corrections with a green pencil. Her English was better than Julius's, but he said it was too perfect. Afterward he would alter half the changes she had made, saying, "It may be good English, but nobody talks that way." The look on Bibi's face as she glanced at the screen seemed to me overly patient, as though "the children," as she called Roma and Michael, were in above their heads. What does it matter now, she seemed to be telling herself. As for me, I went about my business. I never interfered with Roma, and certainly never with Julius in the room. As I watched the program, my allegiances shifted back and forth. Sometimes I hated the men and women who had done something in my name, and sometimes I hated the victims – yes, passionately. It is not normal conversation to talk about old deaths. No matter what was shown on television, no matter what we had to reconsider or see in a new light, my house was large and I had no servant except for an Italian half the day. Even with Bibi helping after work in the evenings, the house was too much for me. I saw that Roma's myths might include misery and sadness, but my myths were bombed, vanished, and whatever remained had to be cleaned and polished and kept bright. At times like these, Bibi seemed to know more than I did. She seemed so lofty, so superior, with her knowledge of hardship, that I wanted to scream at her, "Damn you, Bibi, I saw my mother running, running out of a burning house with her hair on fire. Her hands and face were like black paper when she died." Then the program came to an end and Julius stood before the screen lecturing Michael. He said, "A mission in life – a goal. Without an ideal, life is nothing." He stood with his hands behind his back. He has never smoked, not even when cigarettes were hard to get and everyone craved them. He is frugal, neat; every other day he eats nothing for dinner but yogurt. He said, "These unfortunate people you have just seen had a mission." Michael, the future executive, sat worshipping every word that fell from Julius. "Oh, a highly spiritual mission," said Julius easily. "A goal of a highly – spiritual – nature. That is why they are remembered." Bibi said (had she been drinking too much?), "Encouraging people to buy synthetic products they don't really need will be Michael's mission. Do you think it compares?"

The roof did not cave in. Julius merely laughed. How soft, how easy Julius had become!

"Papa is so short that when he sits down he looks like a little dog begging for sugar," said his beloved Roma, somewhere about that period. Roma had just tasted her first champagne. Julius smiled and touched her bright hair. It was shameful, but once Roma had made that remark about the little dog Julius began appearing in my dreams in that form. He was a terrier who simply would not stop barking. Roma was growing up, but he did not seem jealous. He had, in fact, selected the husband he wanted for her. He chose Michael when Roma was only fourteen or so, and began to train him, and then he went back to having other women again.

The girl and the diary had long been forgotten. Some new person called Julius on the telephone day after day. He trailed the long wire of the bedroom phone to his bathroom. Even Roma would never have dared to listen on an extension; he could smile if Roma was impertinent and pretty and had just drunk a glass of wine, but he could also be frightening. I have never seen anyone outstare him. He would take the phone to the bathroom and talk for a long time. The ringing stopped. In the weeks of lull that followed I dreamed of gunfire, of someone who claimed to be my mother, and of dogs. Julius suddenly ordered me to go with him on a long business journey to Hong Kong, Japan, California, and Vancouver. He said he was sick of travelling alone. I understood that he wanted protection from a woman who had become tiresome – someone who was either over there and waiting, or planning to follow. I remembered the telephone and the peculiar long ring of long-distance calls, the ring that continued after you lifted the receiver. Sometimes I thought I would take Roma and vanish, but the thought never lasted. I did not want to live outside my own house.

"If it is only for the sake of company, then take Bibi," I said. "Roma is at a delicate age. I can't leave her. Bibi has never been anywhere. You said you wanted her to study at one of the Anglo-Saxon universities." He had said that once, but fifteen years ago. However, because the idea had once been his, he now decided it would do Bibi, and thus Possner, some good. There was something else – being honourably rid of her. It was obvious that the idea of travelling with Bibi for company bored him. She was an old friend of the family now, plain and pedantic. He was a busy man with not much time for conversation. He had personal and professional acquaintances in South Africa, Argentina, Sweden, Milan, and many other places I had never seen. He was still very kind to young people if they were worth his while and knew how to make good use of an education. In what manner was he ever less than fair to Bibi? What would Bibi have done without Julius? How many refugees would have given years of their lives to have been in Bibi's place? Julius was very fit. He did yoga exercises every Sunday. I had given in to twin beds, but I refused the idea of separate rooms.

Bibi accepted the interesting journey and the chance to study at an Anglo-Saxon university without thanks and without joy. It meant an interruption of work that interested her, and she was frightened of planes. "It will be like a fairy tale," she said sadly. She must have been remembering stories where little children are abandoned in deep woods by parents who no longer can feed them. She was thinking of dark branches, night, crows spreading their wings, inch-high demons squealing a hideous language.

"Well, of course you are thinking of fairy tales," I said. "But do remember you are a grown woman." I looked at her pale

cheeks and tried to see another Bibi, with spokes of sunflower
hair. She had nothing in common with Julius now except an
adoration for Roma. I had showed her that other girl's diary
and she had been shocked. "An *ignorant* person," she said, and
I saw how little she knew about him. If Bibi herself had not at
one time had the *appearance* of an inferior, if she had not said
"Heidi, you swine!" in a farm girl's accent, then Julius would
never have looked at her twice.

Julius, who was good at arrangements, abandoned Bibi at a
university in the west of Canada and came home alone. Her
wounded, homesick letters followed, one a day. She told about
a sign reading, "Gas at City Prices," which she never understood and which became the symbol of everything she never
would grasp over there. She went to an Italian grocery and
stood weeping because it was Europe. She had knifelike memories of towns and streets. Every girl reminded her of Roma.
She wrote that she had suddenly learned she was old and
plain. Her gestures were awkward; her hair was changing
colour with age. She entered a bookstore and found a shelf of
German poetry. She congratulated the owner, who said, "Oh,
we try" so sarcastically that she knew her accent and her
appearance were offensive. She wanted to answer, but the
English Julius had considered "too perfect" turned out to be
full of holes. She became frightened of shops and when she
went into one she would stand near the door, not daring to
say what she wanted, letting other customers push in front of
her. She stopped a stranger in the street to ask a direction.

"Go to hell," he said. She counted the weeks, days, and minutes until she could be with us again. The first person she embraced at the airport was Roma.

Roma whispered, "Michael thinks he has me, but wait and see. Papa said he could live with us, but I would never let anyone take Aunt Bibi's room."

I heard, and thought, Now I shall have Bibi for the rest of my life.

Was that such a bad prospect? While Bibi had been gaining experience and writing those despairing letters, I had fallen ill. One day Julius asked me to unpack a suitcase for him and I found myself unable to move or speak. This passed, but the attack returned each time Julius gave me an order. The neurologist he sent me to said that my paralytic seizures were caused by nothing more serious than a calcium deficiency. I was instructed to eat sixty grams of cheese four times a day. With Bibi there, I had no more calcium problems. She took over her old duties of ironing and washing the supper dishes – anything the Italian had forgotten or had left undone – and I began reading again. I read fewer books and more magazines. Possner now owned several. It was at Julius's suggestion that a sign was put up in the editorial offices of each saying, "Your readers never went to high school."

Julius was now a colonel, and we moved here, to the newest and best of our homes. It was our house, and Julius put it in my name, as he had promised me long ago. Every windowpane belongs to me.

I knew quite a great deal about Julius; not everything. One summer evening we sat on our terrace, all five of us, with a portable television between us, and the remains of a sunset. Julius went indoors to fetch a bottle of white wine. With two wives and a daughter to serve him he need not have lifted a finger, but he was particular about wine (his cellar is shock-proof and soundproof) and he thought no one else knew how to take the cork out of a bottle. Presently I followed to see if he had everything he needed. He was in the kitchen with a glass of wine in his hand, and he stood sipping it in front of a mirror, deep in silent conversation. "What a good time you and I are having," he might have been saying. He smiled, and his face went wry. "Oh, you know how it is sometimes," he might have said now. He was seducing someone in the mirror – only it was himself. Julius was watching Julius seducing Julius. I remembered how confident he was when he was in love. I went back to the terrace and sat down.

I said, "Julius is a brilliant, clever man." No one answered. That opinion was the rule of the house.

The sunset died; Michael switched on lights hidden in trees and at the bottom of the pool. Waiting for the evening news, we watched, with some disgust, a beer-drinking contest.

"Why show this to us?" said Julius. He had a bouquet of long-stemmed glasses between his fingers. He set the glasses down carefully. "No one here is Bavarian."

"Right," cried Michael. "We are not Bavarian! Roma is not, and her mother is from Dortmund, and Aunt Bibi is from . . . and . . . and *you* are from . . ." He should have known where Julius was born. He must surely have read the vital facts about Julius in Possner house publications often enough. ". . . here, in Cologne," Michael gasped, correctly.

On the screen a slight girl downed a stein of beer in six seconds. Her throat worked in anguish and tension. She turned out to be a Berliner, not a Bavarian, either. She said she had noticed her gift of rapid drinking when still very young. It worked with milk or beer, but not so well with water.

As soon as the news came on, Julius showed signs of annoyance. The conversational aspect of world affairs has always been an irritant to him. What good is talk? In the middle of a remark about the Common Market he turned it off. He said that everyone was incompetent.

Michael the sycophant said, "Why don't you send very efficient well-trained men from Possner into politics? You could take someone promising and give him a sound education and launch him in a good party – in fact, you could launch several in all parties. Then no matter who was elected you would be certain everything would run efficiently. . . ." He always let his sentences run down. Even when a sentence normally might have come to a stop, it sounded as if the end were nowhere. Sometimes my future son-in-law looked like a terrier too, peering from one large human to the other, wondering who would slip him a morsel of something good.

"Wouldn't that strike you as immoral, Michael?" Here was Bibi sitting in the shadows – lumpy, wearing heavy stockings, saying prickly, difficult things. Bibi is raving, I thought. It seemed to me that the girl's voice had grown rasping. A "girl," I called her, but the person determined to spoil our enjoyment of the summer weather was nearly forty, had popping blue eyes, and had failed as an emigrant.

As if Bibi's remark weren't enough, now impertinent Roma spoke up: "You aren't much of a generation to talk about morality." This was annoying, for it meant she was mixing up the generations and making us older than we really were.

Bibi laughed and said, "Little girl, what do you know about some of us?"

"Enough of that," said Julius, who did not need to shout to be frightening. "Enough from Bibi. Bibi, don't you dare touch my daughter's innocence."

My heart was pounding. For the first time I felt that Julius and I were thinking as one. Our marriage was our house. I said to myself, "Here we are together in the fortress. The bodies pile up outside. Don't look at them." I forgave him for Bibi, the girl of the diary, the twin beds, the long-distance calls, for being a peacock who preened before mirrors. I put a hundred injuries and injustices behind me.

Bibi had pushed her chair back and risen and, after hesitating, looking over our heads and all round the garden, she walked away, down the sloping lawn. The pool, the trees, the imported white camellias in pots, were beautifully lighted. We – particularly Roma – had looked charming, I thought, and now here was one person walking out of the picture. Michael suddenly said, "The neighbours!" and pressed a switch – a foolish gesture that left us sitting in semidarkness. Later he said he thought Bibi was about to drown herself in the pool and that our neighbours, excited by the sound of a quarrel (What sound? We were speaking quietly), might peer at us through field glasses.

"Turn the lights on immediately," said Julius, without moving.

We saw Roma clinging to Bibi and we heard her sobbing, "I didn't mean you, I meant everybody else."

"Now they have made my daughter cry on a lovely summer evening," said Julius, but quite casually, as if it were only one complaint on a long list of misdemeanours. But we were able to laugh, finally, because Michael, in his anxiety, had pressed all the buttons he could find, causing the gate in the driveway to slide back and forth, the garage doors to open and shut, and the pool in the garden to blink like a star. The lilies on the surface of the pool flashed negative-positive-negative. (It was thanks to an idea of Bibi's that Julius had been able to grow the lilies; their roots feed on a chemical mixture encased in a sphere. Even with flowers the pool looks sterile. I always found the water lilies unpleasant; they attract dragonflies.) I had a vision that cramped my stomach, of Bibi face down among the negative-positive lilies, with dragonflies darting at her wet hair.

Bibi now let Roma lead her back to us. Julius poured wine as if nothing had happened, and he answered Michael's question. He said, "An idea similar to yours was discussed, but we have decided against it." We all let Julius have the last word.

Bibi finally died in America, by gas. She had gone out to an American branch of Possner at her own request. She left her passport and bankbook and some loose money on her kitchen table. The money was weighed down with the marble darning egg I had brought her from Italy years before. She named Julius as her closest living relative and Roma as her direct heir. There was also a sealed letter for Julius, which the police had opened before he arrived. Julius flew over, of course, though he was not a relative. After twenty years of Bibi we still did not know if she had any real family. In the letter she said she willed her body to a medical school, but since she also said she hoped there was enough money on the table to pay for a modest funeral, no one could tell exactly what she had wanted. Because of the circumstances there was a police autopsy. Julius brought back a photocopy of her letter – the police kept the original. Instead of telling why she had wanted to kill herself Bibi explained that she had chosen early morning so that she would be discovered at some time during the day and not after dark. She knew of accidents that had been caused by someone's turning on a light in a room filled with gas. I said to Julius that all she needed to have done was turn off the electricity; there must have been a switch somewhere in the apartment. But no, said Julius, Bibi had probably thought of that too. What if she remained alone and undiscovered for days, as she had after that first failed mess of a try with gardénal? Some stranger might have broken down the door, tried a light, and, failing to find one, might have absent-mindedly struck a match. This sounded involved, not very sensible. Actually, she was found in broad daylight and no one was hurt.

Later, much later, on an evening when Julius was in a pleasant mood, I asked him about that girl's diary – if he knew how it had come to be on the shelf of a linen cupboard. It took him minutes to understand what I was talking about, and then he said the diary belonged to a silly uneducated person. He could not recall anything about a shelf. He was certain, in fact, that he had thrown the diary, unread, in a wastebasket.

"What did she mean by 'everything'?" I said.

He did not remember.

"You can see how unimportant she was," Julius said. "I wanted to have nothing to do with her, and so she sent me the diary so I could read about her soul. We are discussing an imaginary situation. There was no evidence that I was involved. My name was not mentioned anywhere," Julius concluded.

We were sitting on the terrace during this conversation. Julius, not yet fifty, had been made a general, and we drank to his triumph and his life. I had the nausea and dizziness of the repeated moment, as though we had sat in exactly the same position once before and I had heard Julius explain the same portion of his past. I saw the water lilies.

"I have dreams about Bibi," I said.

"She had an incurable illness," he replied.

This had never been mentioned. The water lilies seemed enormous. "Was it in the autopsy report?"

"Naturally."

Divinities invent convenient fables, but they are never mistaken. It must have been true; Bibi had an incurable illness and died to spare herself useless pain. Our conversation could have ended there, since we had no further use for it. Unfortunately I had still another question.

"That first time," I said. "The first time you travelled over there with Bibi for company and left her and came back alone. You remember? The day you were to leave, something happened. I was in the living room with Roma when we heard shrieks of hysterical laughter from the hall. Roma ran out ahead of me and began to scream in the same strident way. Bibi was in front of the looking glass trying on a hat. It was a hat specially bought for the journey. An ignoble hat. A disgusting and hideous hat of cheap turquoise jersey. She had no taste – any salesgirl could fob off anything. The salesgirl had told her she had a bad hairline, and this criminal hat covered her head from the eyebrows to the nape of her neck. Michael the subaltern, having already seen that you were laughing, was doubled up, yelling, outdoing himself in laughter. You said to Bibi, 'I shall take you to a corner of the airport where the wind can blow it away.' Roma – she was fifteen or sixteen – said, 'Aunt Bibi looks like a little piglet dressed up as an actress.' At that, Bibi, who had been laughing too, moved away from the mirror and said, 'That was unkind.' All at once you saw I was not laughing at all. You turned and knelt down to buckle a suitcase as if the scene did not concern you any more. Bibi was finished then. Michael had felt the shift of power too. *I* mattered."

All this had been meant to lead up to a question, but I had lost it. Anyway, Julius had stopped listening almost from the beginning. He sipped his wine and looked attentive, but his thoughts were floating. In the same voice, as if continuing my boring anecdote, I said, ". . . and tigers and zebras and ants and bees . . ."

"Yes, yes," said Julius, pretending to hear.

"Oh, Julius, Julius," I said in the same voice. "Now a general, tomorrow a field marshal. Last night in a dream I had you were nothing but a little dog who kept on barking, and Bibi had to thrash you to make you stop."

© Alison Harris

Born in Montreal in 1922, Mavis Gallant left a career as a leading journalist in that city to move to Paris in 1950 to write.

Since that time she has been publishing stories on a regular basis in *The New Yorker*, many of which have been anthologized. Her world-wide reputation has been established by books such as *From the Fifteenth District* and *Home Truths*, which won the Governor General's Award in 1982. In that same year she was made an Officer of the Order of Canada, becoming a Companion of the Order in 1993, the year that she published *Across the Bridge* and was the recipient of a special tribute at the Harbourfront International Festival of Authors in Toronto. In 1996, *The Selected Stories of Mavis Gallant* was published to universal acclaim.

Gallant is a Foreign Honorary Member of the American Academy of Arts and Letters, and Fellow of the Royal Society of Literature. She has received several honorary degrees from Canadian universities and remains a much-sought-after public speaker. In 2001 she became the first winner of the Matt Cohen Award, and in 2002 she was awarded the Blue Metropolis International Literary Grand Prix and the Rea Award for the Short Story.

She continues to live in Paris.